Super Me, Too

BOOK 2

Ray Wenck

Glory Days Press

Columbus, Ohio

Copyright © 2019 by Ray Wenck

Ray Wenck
www.raywenck.com

Book Layout © 2016 BookDesignTemplates.com

Book Title/ Author Name. -- 1st ed.
ISBN 978-1-7331918-4-5

Dedicated to all the special Super Mes I've had the joy of working with over the years.

Acknowledgement

I'd like to thank all those committed to working with, caring for, and educating the beautiful special needs children of the world. Bless you for your time, patience and love. It's not always easy but in those moments when their eyes light and the smile spreads across their faces all is made right.

Thank you to Jodi McDermitt for her usual masterful work at making this story the best it can be.

Thanks to Ren McKenzie for his creative cover design.

I have a special love for this character. If you want to see more of Nathan and Ker-sey let me know. Thanks to you, the reader for all the support over the past. Your comments and reviews are appreciated.

As always, read all you want, I'll write more.

CHAPTER ONE

Janelle's hand shook as she picked up the phone. She didn't want to make the call, but she had no one else. She reminded herself she wasn't making the call for herself. It was for Nathan, her twelve-year-old Down syndrome son. He needed special care, stability, a routine, and to be in the company of someone who understood his needs to make sure he was protected.

She scrolled down the numbers. It had been more than a month since she last saw him. His number may no longer be in the call log. No, there it was. A moment of sadness tweaked her already somber mood. She didn't know enough people or receive enough calls for the log to be full, let alone a number to be dropped from the list.

She stared at the number. It may not be good anymore. If he was what she suspected, wasn't changing phones on a regular basis part of the norm? Even if the phone was still active, he might not answer. After all, she'd made it quite clear that he was no longer welcome around her son. Why would he answer?

But she had a problem. She was having surgery. She'd be in the hospital for at least one night. Nathan had nowhere to stay. She had no other close relatives. A few friends, yes, but none she trusted enough or were willing to care for Nathan, even for a short time.

She tried to get the hospital to allow him to stay in her room, but once they learned he was a special needs child, that idea was dismissed. The nurses and other staff did not need the extra responsibility of watching him on top of their other duties. Besides, he could be a disruption to the other patients.

They were quick enough to suggest other services, but that was no different than leaving him with a stranger. Not that Kersey wasn't a stranger too. After all, she had only met him but the instant connection with Nathan told her a lot about the large muscular man.

She pressed the number and closed her eyes. She thought about praying but couldn't decide if it was for him to pick up or not, so she ignored the urge. One ring. Two. Was it disappointment she felt, or relief? Three. Four. Her heart sank. She opened her eyes. She was surprised to find them blurry. She sighed and moved the phone away from her ear. As she moved to end the call, his voice came through the speaker.

"Hello?" He sounded anxious. Was that a note of excitement? "Hello? Are you still there?"

Janelle cleared her suddenly dry throat. "Yeah. Yes, I'm still here. I was about to hang up. I-I wasn't sure you'd answer."

"Sorry. I was in the shower."

She refused to allow that image to play in her mind.

"Is everything all right? Is Nathan okay?"

"Yes, he's fine."

"And you?" His voice was less anxious, almost tender.

She swallowed hard and closed her eyes to hold back the tears. She failed. "No. I'm not doing so well." The sob erupted. It was so unexpected she was unable to prevent it.

"What is it?"

"I, uh, I have to go in for surgery." She hadn't realized how scared she was until that moment. She had no one to talk to about her problems. Other than to tell her boss she needed time off, she hadn't told anyone. The thought saddened her more and the tears fell heavier. Janelle could not speak, but he kept talking.

"If you need me to come, I'll be there. I have something I have to finish first, but I will come."

"O-kay," she managed between sobs. "I'm sorry. I have no one else to call. I know you'll take good care of Nathan until I'm home."

"You can count on me. How soon do you need me?"

This was the hard part. She had waited too long to call, either afraid of his answer or that he wouldn't take the call in the first place. "I go in tomorrow morning."

"Tomorrow!"

"If you can't do it, I understand. I'll figure something out. I'm sorry to have bothered you."

"No! Wait! I've got this, uh, thing to do. If I can take care of it tonight, I'll be there."

"Okay. I can get someone to take Nathan to school, so you won't have to be here until three. I'll leave the key under the door mat."

"No, not there. It's too obvious. Put it on the back porch somewhere."

"Okay. I have a list of things Nathan needs. Do you want me to email it to you?"

"Ah, no. I don't have an email account. Just leave a note there."

"I really appreciate you doing this—for Nathan. I'm sorry for the way I spoke to you last time. I was scared. You know, for Nathan."

"I understood."

She hesitated, wanting to say more, but changed her mind. "So, I can count on you being here tomorrow?" She cringed, hoping she hadn't just insulted him.

"I promise. I'll send you a text as soon as I'm at the house."

"Okay. Thank you."

"Janelle?"

"Yes?"

"Are you okay?"

"I will be now that I know Nathan is taken care of."

Silence. It added weight to the phone. She didn't want to explain. She didn't want to think about how serious it might be, or that Nathan might be left alone. "Thanks again. Goodbye." She disconnected. Set the phone down. Stared at it. Then covered her face as she broke into tears.

CHAPTER TWO

Kersey stared at the phone. The call was not expected. Ever. Janelle must be in a tight spot if she was willing to forgive him for putting Nathan in jeopardy. He hoped she'd be all right and vowed to do his best for Nathan. The phone buzzed in his hand. A text from Aleeyah. *Where r u?*

He was late, distracted from his mission by the surprise phone call. *Coming.* He broke into a run to make up the time. It wasn't the smartest thing to do when trying to remain inconspicuous, but he couldn't leave his partner stranded to face The Snake alone.

They had been hired by a wealthy businessman from Kansas City to rescue his daughter from a cult. The young woman had already been returned, but the cult leader had hooked her on a designer drug created to make the addict happy and compliant. Under questioning she gave up her personal and financial information. Her accounts were stripped bare and her identity sold. The young woman was now in an intensive rehab facility. The father was furious. He rehired Kersey to take the man down so he could not take advantage of anyone else.

Aleeyah was posing as a potential new cult member. The initial contact had already been made. Now she was being met by the boss, a sleazy man known as The Snake for his ability to slither out of danger and any traps set by law enforcement. As soon as he cleaned out enough cult members, The Snake packed up and moved to a new location in a different state and started again.

Kersey was supposed to record the meeting, then follow as they brought Aleeyah to the new cult grounds. The Snake travelled with an entourage that was large both in numbers and size. The four men that served as his personal bodyguards were every bit as large as Kersey, if not bigger. Six other well-trained men acted as security for the cult locations. A staff of eight handled the daily business, including a chef, a personal assistant, a yoga instructor, and an event planner.

Since leaving Nathan and Janelle a month ago, he and Aleeyah had moved across the country taking various jobs. This was their fourth mission together. He liked her. She was professional, tough, skilled, and attractive. But now, he was late. He had to get to the spot he'd selected before The Snake and his men arrived.

He ran along the grass-covered knoll at full speed. One slip and he'd be rolling down the slope. He reached the line of trees and slowed. The knoll ran the length of a park. The other side was bordered by a river. A playground stood to the right. Below him was a parking lot. Between the lot and the river was an open shelter house, tennis and basketball courts, and a skate park. Picnic tables dotted the ground along the shore.

He pressed against a tree and aimed the binoculars downhill. "Nonononono," he repeated in a panic. Aleeyah was not in sight. He'd missed her. Now what would he do?

Wait! There she was. He spotted her purple hair in the back seat of a large Lincoln Town Car. She sat between two bodyguards. The Snake was turned around in the passenger seat speaking to Aleeyah. The car backed out of the spot. A second vehicle, a black SUV, held the other two bodyguards.

Kersey lifted the camera, zoomed in, and videoed the Town Car as it drove away. He didn't get as much video evidence as he'd wanted, but at least he could verify she was with The Snake. He **shut the camera off and sprinted back the way he'd just come.**

He reached the SUV that was almost a half mile away in record time, at least for him. Knowing his partner was out of sight for that long worried him. He could not let them get her alone where they could drug her. She'd fight, that was for sure, but even her extreme skills might not be enough to overcome the bodyguards.

Unless they were suspicious of her, Kersey thought they'd wait to get her to the compound. Perhaps lull her with food and drink before pouncing. Of course, if they were on to her, they wouldn't risk taking her to the compound. They'd find somewhere more secluded where they could interrogate and then dispose of her. He couldn't let that happen.

Kersey fired up the engine and peeled from the parking spot. They'd created a back story for her that would survive a cursory examination, but anyone with skills could expose the ruse. As he sped toward the route they'd take to the compound, he couldn't shake the thought.

He reached the expressway, gauging how much of a lead they had and how long it should take for him to catch sight of them. At the top of the ramp he strained his vision, but if they were there, he didn't see them. He barreled down the ramp, entering the expressway doing eighty. He cut in front of a semi, the driver letting him know his irritation with a long blast of the horn.

The compound was twenty miles from the meeting place. He figured he should see them by the time they reached their exit, however math had never been one of his strong subjects. At least that's what he told himself when he reached the exit without a glimpse of the two-vehicle caravan.

On more empty roads, Kersey pushed the pedal down. He had to know she made it. She had to be safe. He was almost hyperventilating when he reached the compound. Kersey had to force his foot from the pedal to slow down for a drive by and prevent the urge to ram the ornate gate.

The SUV crawled by the massive estate. The long driveway was partially concealed by trees lining the front fence. He caught just enough of a glimpse to determine the Town Car was not there. In a rage, he pounded the steering wheel. He whirled the SUV around, cutting off a minivan to another chorus of horn blasts, then sped back the way he came.

His entire body popped sweat beads. He pulled the cell phone out and punched in Aleeyah's number. They had a predetermined dialogue. He'd say, "It's your brother, Benny." She'd reply one of two ways. Either, "Hi Benny, I can't talk now. I'll call you later," which meant everything was all right. Or she'd say, "I don't have a brother. You have the wrong number," which meant get your butt there as fast as possible. Either answer allowed her to turn on the locator in her phone. Fearing she might be scanned, she turned it off for the meet.

The phone rang and rang and rang. Damn! The steering wheel received more punishment. He pulled over. He had one other way of tracking her, but he had to use his computer to access remote activation. The problem with that was it either pinged or vibrated the phone, depending whether the ringer was on or silenced.

He went to work as fast as his beefy fingers allowed. He connected, activated, and waited as the program searched for the phone. An agonizing two minutes later, he was zeroed in. Kersey retraced his route back to the expressway. The caravan continued straight. That was all the confirmation he needed that Aleeyah was in trouble. Speed was important. He pushed the pedal down, the needle passing one hundred. Two exits further up, he turned off. His turn was fast and wide, but this was a less populated area and there were no oncoming cars. The SUV teetered on the brink of tipping. Kersey fought hard, bleeding off speed for stability. Once righted, he pressed the pedal to the floor again.

He glanced at the computer to get his bearings. The phone was no longer moving. Was that good or bad? It had to be bad. If they were still moving, Aleeyah was still okay. Once they stopped, the trouble would begin.

The gap between him and the phone closed fast. He made a turn and the phone was down the road less than a mile. That couldn't be right. He could easily see that far ahead, and there were no other vehicles. A chill ran up his spine and a knot as hard and explosive as a mortar shell formed in his stomach. Had they killed Aleeyah and dumped her body? No. He couldn't, wouldn't accept that.

He slowed as he closed on the spot. Nothing. It was a large open field with tall unkempt grass and weeds. Kersey got out, fearing what he might find. He stood on the berm and scanned the area. A drainage ditch ran along the road. He slid down into it. No body. He climbed to the top on the opposite side. Nothing. He kicked around at the knee-high growth. His search took five minutes to be sure Aleeyah was not there. So where was she?

He looked down the road. A mile farther, trees took over the landscape. He'd check there. He slid down the slope of the ditch. As he crossed the bottom, his foot kicked something. He bent and discovered a phone. He recognized the Hello Kitty designer case. Aleeyah's.

He'd lost her.

CHAPTER THREE

No, he had to keep searching. Kersey sprinted up the far side, jumped into the SUV, and shot ahead. He slowed as he reached the trees. It would be a perfect place to hide a body, but the ditch made driving across it impossible. He continued on. With each passing mile the dread squeezed his heart tighter. An intersection ahead made decisions harder. Too much time had passed already.

To the right was open ground for as far as he could see. The left offered a more scenic route with trees and a small rise, but a green sign said a town was three miles away. Kersey eliminated that route. The Snake wouldn't want to risk being seen by a random driver. He eyed straight ahead. Scattered trees and open ground. His gut flipped. He took that as a sign and drove straight.

Once more the needle touched one hundred. The land passed in a blur. He passed a copse of trees and caught a glint of sunlight reflecting off something within. He braked hard. The tires screeched like they'd been frightened by a demon. The SUV swayed right then left. Kersey fought the wheel to prevent flipping. At such a high speed, survival was unlikely.

Instead of coming to a complete stop, he angled off road and bounced wildly over the uneven landscape. The maneuver was so fast, he was only half sure there was no ditch. He steered the SUV toward the trees. He stopped fifty yards short, exploded from the seat and ran with gun in hand and a prayer on his lips.

As he reached the tree line, a shot echoed from somewhere inside. He ducked, thinking the shot was intended for him. A second one told him the shots were meant for someone else. Aleeyah! Hang on, girl, I'm coming. He rounded the tree in a crouch and made his way through woods. The sound of fist striking flesh gave him a direction. He moved left.

Voices. "Hold her, man. There's four of you, for God's sake." It had to be The Snake.

Kersey advanced fast, concerned more with speed than stealth.

"That's it. Keep her pinned."

Kersey throttled up, fearing he'd be too late. He burst into a small clearing. The Town car and the SUV were parked to the right. The driver of the Lincoln was still inside. The Snake stood on the far side of where three men struggled to hold Aleeyah down. A fourth man had a gun leveled at Aleeyah. His sudden appearance caused everyone to shift their gazes from her to him. For a moment, the entire woods went silent, then Kersey fired three shots. The man with gun dropped. The other three men scrambled for weapons. The Snake bugged out, his long legs churning toward the car.

Aleeyah whipped her muscular legs, connecting with the face of the thug by her feet. He flew back and she was up. Kersey placed a three-round burst into another man as he aimed his gun at the back of Aleeyah's head.

In two blurred moves, Aleeyah disarmed the last man and fired point blank into his surprised face.

A crash drew their attention. In his panic to get away, the driver of the Lincoln reversed into the SUV as The Snake ran after the car. He screamed at the driver to wait, but the driver was more afraid of Aleeyah and Kersey than of his boss. The car swung around to get past the SUV, but the long body made the turn too wide. As the reverse lights came on to allow for a better angle, Kersey fired into the tires, blowing out the two on the passenger side. The driver flew from the car like he'd been ejected and ran screaming through the woods. Kersey let him go.

Aleeyah marched toward The Snake with murderous intent. Kersey couldn't blame her, but the goal was to bring the sleazeball to justice. Still, he couldn't stop her. She deserved to extract some revenge.

The Snake backed away, hands up to stop her advance. "No. No, please. I wasn't going to hurt you. Just scare you a little. Honest."

"Yeah, me too." She took a quick short step to set up her kick. Her long leg flashed up, connecting under The Snake's meaty chin.

The force snapped his head back, lifting his body from the ground. He arched backward and fell hard.

Kersey watched the strike, mouth agape. It was a toss-up which had killed him; the neck snapping back or his head cracking on the tree root. To his surprise, the man rolled to his side, moaned, and went sleepytime.

Kersey slid the gun back in the holster and approached Aleeyah. She whirled on him, fire in her eyes. "Where were you?" She took a threatening step toward him. He stopped moving.

"I'm sorry. I got delayed."

"What could possibly have delayed you while you were on a mission, especially one where my life was on the line?"

Kersey winced, knowing she wouldn't like the answer. "I, uh, got a phone call."

Aleeyah's eyes lit like a winning sledgehammer game at a carnival. "A what?"

"Yeah, that was bad. I'm sorry."

"Let me get this straight. With my life in peril, you stop to take a phone call? Are you completely nuts? Who could've possibly called that was more important than me, your trusted partner?"

"Ah, well, it was Janelle."

"Janelle! The woman who chased you from her house and out of her son's life? Really? She is more important to you than me?"

"No, of course not. But..."

She held up a hand. "Unh-uh. There is no but. You chose Janelle. That can't fly. How can I ever trust you again?"

"Aleeyah, come on. It was a mistake. It won't happen again."

"You can bet it won't, 'cause we're done."

She walked away, trailing fumes.

CHAPTER FOUR

Aleeyah refused to speak to him on the way back. After loading The Snake into the back seat, the frost settled over the vehicle. Kersey worked hard to apologize and draw her out, but she folded her arms across her chest and turned her cold eyes toward the window.

Kersey had placed his gun in The Snake's hand and pulled the trigger a few times. He called 911 from the dead man's phone, then deposited his unconscious body where he would easily be found when the police arrived. A second call from a burner phone described the shoot-out in the woods.

Done, Kersey made one final attempt to change Aleeyah's mind, but she cut him off. "Just drop me off at the hotel."

Which was what he did.

"I have to meet with the client. I'll be back in an hour. Please. Let's talk then." She gave him a cool gaze, then a quick nod before exiting the SUV. He left feeling encouraged.

The client was happy and vowed to make the agreed upon deposit into Kersey's account once word of The Snake's capture was aired. Satisfied, Kersey returned to the hotel, rehearsing what he wanted to say to Aleeyah. He liked her and enjoyed working as a team. This business was not an easy one and finding a partner you could rely on and trust was difficult. He vowed to make it up to her. However, when he knocked on her door there was no answer. On a hunch he went to the front desk to discover she already checked out. She'd left a note. He had hope that given time, she might reconsider, but the note said simply, "Deposit my share into the usual account."

Deflated, Kersey withdrew to his room and crashed on the bed. He'd blown it. Her leaving was his fault and without knowing how to contact her, Kersey had no way to convince her to give him a second chance. Tired and depressed, he wanted to sleep for a long time. Instead, he packed his duffel bag, checked out, and headed east to his babysitting job.

After a while, he successfully pushed his failure aside with thoughts of Nathan and Janelle. Despite his mood, he had to smile as funny images of Nathan came back to him. The happy round face. The way his eyes closed when he beamed his big toothy smile. The way he pronounced his name. "Ker-sey."

And of course, the wild yellow super hero suit with the red cape and the large S with the word *Me* underneath. The visual of Nathan running around the yard in that costume with the cape flying behind him evoked a laugh.

Then his mood darkened as he remembered the danger he'd put Nathan in, getting him kidnapped by a Russian gangster. His fear for Nathan's life caused him to use his power. He seldom revealed his ability, but in that situation he had no choice. He'd cut it loose with no concern of the damage or lives taken. His only concern was saving Nathan.

Then a new thought came to him; one he'd wondered about ever since the encounter in the warehouse. The vision of Nathan in the chair, levitating from the floor. It had not been Kersey. But he'd been unable to ask Nathan about the strange occurrence. Did the boy have some innate ability of his own? If so, how had he come by it? Did he even know he had the power, and could he control it?

Another remembrance of that night surfaced. Aleeyah standing in the doorway. How long had she been there? Had she witnessed the destruction he unleashed? If so, she never mentioned it, nor did he ask her. Something strange had happened in that warehouse. He planned on asking Nathan about it, but would he even remember? Only one way to find out.

He pushed through the night, eventually stopping at a small mom and pop motel. He needed to arrive no later than two in the afternoon the next day to retrieve the key, read Janelle's instructions, and be on time to pick up Nathan. Kersey was pleased to find he was looking forward to seeing the young boy again. He was equally as determined not to let Nathan's mother down.

Kersey arrived an hour early. Before parking, he cruised the neighborhood as more of a precaution than a fear. He had history there and it paid to be cautious.

Finding no one threatening or suspicious, Kersey parked the SUV a block down the street and walked to the house. He was armed for the moment, but knew he'd have to give up his weapon once Nathan was around. Not wanting to look like a burglar, he didn't pass by the house and then double back. Instead, he turned up the driveway like he belonged there.

At the back of the house he found the key Janelle left buried an inch deep in a flower pot. As he bent to retrieve it, the fragrance of the purple flowers wafted to his nostrils. The pleasing scent drew him closer for a deeper inhalation. It reminded him of Janelle. The thought brought a warm sensation that he basked in for a moment. He glanced around to see if anyone had noticed his strange behavior.

He inserted the key and entered, pausing on the threshold to listen. Then, he stepped in and closed the door gently before pulling his gun. Force of habit did not allow him to enter a building without clearing it first. He treaded softly through the kitchen, bathroom, dining room, and front room before descending into the basement. All was clear.

He crept up the stairs to the second floor, placing his feet to one side of the steps and keeping his eyes and gun scanning upward. The house was small with not many places to hide. He cleared the two bedrooms and the bathroom. Satisfied he was alone, he breathed easier and returned to the main floor.

On the dining room table was a legal pad. *Kersey* was written in big letters at the top of the first page. *Thank you again for doing this. I should only be away for one night. Here is a list of dos and don'ts. Please follow them. There is a reason for each one. I have also included his schedule from after school until bedtime, as well as how to wake him and prepare him for school. Please don't alter the schedule because it throws Nathan off. He has trouble dealing with change. Routine is very important to his mental health.*

A list of his favorite activities is on the next page. He is allowed to watch some television, but no more than an hour. It is important that he stay active and not just sit. Bedtime is very strict. If you let him stay up longer, and he will try to convince you, you will have trouble getting him up in the morning.

If you have any problems, call me. I may not be awake but keep trying. I will call you before his bedtime to say goodnight to him. Thanks again for doing this. J.

The dos and don'ts list was long. Kersey read it twice, then set it down. He had a lot to remember, but how hard could it be? He was just one boy, and they got along well. Besides, it was only for one night, and doing this might go a long way to bridging the gap between Janelle and him.

Yep, a piece of cake. He glanced at the list and the doubts crept in.

CHAPTER FIVE

Kersey checked the clock on the wall. Time to go get Nathan. Not sure she could answer the phone, he texted Janelle to let her know he was on the job. If she needed to, she'd call him back. He locked the back door and exited through the front, then retreated back inside, took the holstered gun from his belt, and set it inside the cabinet above the refrigerator. He left feeling drastically underdressed. He decided to walk the four blocks to school.

The weather was nice; not too hot, and with a clear sky. The closer he got to the school, the more excited he grew to see Nathan. It had only been a little more than a month, so Kersey didn't expect much change, but the boy had been through a lot of trauma the last time they were together. Something like that could alter a trained professional's mindset, let alone a young boy with special needs.

He rounded the corner, crossed the street, and followed the chain link fence surrounding the playground. Janelle's note said Nathan would come out the side door. It was just ahead. A group of parents, mostly women, were already gathered there.

Upon seeing him, a few of them blanched and backed away. Several mouths dropped open, but two of them smiled and looked him over. He avoided them. Kersey was not easy to miss. He towered over everyone in the group. His muscular physique was well defined, though he moved with the grace of a dancer. His almost golden hair was longer than usual, and he swept it back from his face. He glanced at one of the two drooling women and saw she had moved closer. She caught his eye and winked. Though meant to be alluring, it sent a chill down his spine. He took a large step sideways.

A sudden presence next to him had him on edge. His eyes wandered to the side, but he kept his face forward. How had this woman gotten so close without him noticing? Beads of sweat dotted his forehead.

"Hi there, big man." Her voice had practiced seductiveness. "I haven't seen you here before. Are you new to the neighborhood?"

Without looking at her, Kersey said, "Ah, no, just doing a favor for a friend."

"Oh? Which friend?"

Kersey worked hard for an answer that would put an end to the conversation. He was saved from replying when the dismissal bell rang. A sigh of relief escaped him. He jumped when she touched him.

"My, you're a jumpy one, aren't you? And so strong too." She squeezed his bicep.

Kersey swore he heard purring.

"I'm Martha," she said, rolling the r. "What's your name?"

The side door burst open and a group of older kids ran free. The next two classes were younger grade levels and much more orderly in their exit. The teachers stood to the side observing the exodus with watchful eyes.

There was a gap in students, leaving Kersey to wonder if he was at the wrong door. Then the doors opened again and he realized the woman was still fondling his bicep. He glanced down. Her steel grey eyes sparkled and she winked again. He tried to smile, but his lips quivered with the effort.

"Oh, you're nervous. Isn't that adorable? Maybe we should get a drink so I can relax you."

"Ah..." He spotted Nathan. "Oh, there he is. I have to go."

"Okay. See you later?" Her voice was tinged with hope.

"Ah..."

He stepped forward and her nails drew lines across his arm. Kersey walked toward Nathan. A woman he took to be his teacher held Nathan's hand. She spotted him before Nathan did. Her eyes widened and her head tilted backward to look at his face.

"Ker-sey!" Nathan bellowed and tried to run to him, but his teacher did not let go. She pulled him back and said something to him Kersey did not hear.

In a formal voice, she said, "And who are you?"

"I'm here to pick up Nathan."

"That doesn't answer my question. I asked who you are."

"Oh, sorry. I'm Kersey. A friend of Nathan and his mother."

"Nathan, do you know this person?"

"Yuh."

"Who is he?"

"Ker-sey. He is superhero." He shouted, "Superhero!" and swung his free hand up and out to the side. The teacher hesitated. Kersey reached behind him. As his hand came forward, the teacher flinched and took an involuntary step back, pulling Nathan into a protective hold. Kersey hesitated, then offered, "I can show you some ID if you'd like." The woman was being careful with Nathan's safety. Kersey respected that.

He opened his billfold to display his driver's license. She was hesitant to take her gaze from him, but eventually looked down. She seemed to relax.

"I'm sorry, but I can't be too careful in these situations."

"Understood, and I appreciate your efforts on Nathan's behalf."

"His mother called this morning and informed the school that someone would be picking Nathan up today, though I dare say a description would have been, ah, very helpful."

Kersey smiled. The sincerity of his expression soothed her concerns even more. She offered a hand. "I'm Mrs. Wilson. I'm sure you have surmised I'm Nathan's teacher."

Kersey accepted the hand, careful not to press too tight. His hand enveloped hers completely. "Kersey. Nice to meet you."

"Nathan, do you want to go with Kersey?"

"Yuh."

"Very well." To Kersey, she said, "I am officially giving control over to you." She made a show of placing Nathan's hand in his. "Nice to meet you, Kersey. I'll see you tomorrow, Nathan."

"K. Bye." He waved at her, then turned his happy face up to Kersey. He flashed a smile. His eyes closed and his face scrunched up, just like Kersey remembered. He was wearing a red Spiderman backpack that didn't appear to have much inside. That was good, since one of the things on Janelle's list was *Do homework*.

"It's good to see you, Nathan."

"Yuh."

"Are you ready to go home?'

"Yuh."

"We're going to have fun, aren't we?"

"Yuh."

Wanting to get more than a one word response, he said, "What would you like to do?"

He threw his hand in the air and shouted, "Be superheroes!"

The bicep grabber walked by, holding hands with two young girls . "Hmm! I'd like to find a superhero. Would you come rescue me?"

"Ah…"

CHAPTER SIX

On the walk home, Nathan kept staring up at Kersey. They swung their joined hands in big arcs front to back. At the end of the first block, Kersey pulled Nathan back from stepping into the street. "Whoa, buddy. What are you supposed to do before crossing the street?"

His expression grew confused. He creased his brow and tilted his head to the side. "I not buddy. I Nathan."

"Yes, I know, but you didn't answer the question. What are you, Nathan, supposed to do before crossing the street?"

He gave that some thought, perhaps recalling the information. "Look both ways," he blurted with pride.

"Exactly. But you didn't look, did you? If a car came by, it might not be able to stop in time. You might get hit. Let's look together."

They looked left. Nathan spoke in a low voice to himself. "No cars."

They looked right. "No cars."

Kersey looked left again and felt Nathan tug on his hand as the boy stepped into the street. Kersey decided not to say anything this time. Instead, he rewarded the success. "There you go. Nice job."

"Yuh. I smart."

"Yes, you are."

"I know. I told you."

Kersey laughed.

They proceeded down the next block, again going through the street crossing routine. This time Kersey added, "And look left one more time."

They crossed.

They resumed the arm swings.

"Ker-sey. You still superhero?"

"I'm no superhero. You are."

"Yuh. But Ker-sey is too."

"What kind of super powers do you have?" The question had an ulterior motive. He wanted to know if Nathan would admit to having abilities. Of course, he might not be aware of them or how they work.

"Ah, flying."

"Flying? That's a good one. What else."

"Strong." He stopped, rounded his shoulders, and flexed like a pro wrestler. "Yuh. Me strong."

Kersey laughed. "Yes, you are."

"I stronger than you."

"I don't doubt it."

Nathan took Kersey's hand again. They reached the next street. Kersey watched. Nathan stopped, gave a cursory glance in both directions, then looked up with his scrunched up smile. He pointed a finger at his head. "Smart."

"Yes. You are smart and strong."

They stepped off the curb and were halfway across the street when a car barreled toward them. Kersey didn't think the car was going to stop, so he hustled Nathan to the other side and whirled on the car. It screeched to a stop, sticking out into crossing traffic. A man leaned out the passenger window. "Keep that tard outta the road, muscle head."

Anger pulsed inside his head. Kersey saw red and took a threatening step toward the car. He froze, remembering he had Nathan with him.

"Oh, you're so scary," the passenger said. "Go home before you get hurt."

"Bad man," Nathan said.

"Yeah, he's a bad man, or at least thinks he is. Come on, Nathan, let's get home."

Behind him he heard a car door open. Without looking, he knew what was coming. The fool was a bully. He thought he'd rub it in Kersey's face. Big mistake. He had no problem putting this fool down, especially after his inappropriate comment about Nathan. He deserved everything he was about to get.

"Hey, big man. Big scary man. Did you have something you wanted to say to me? 'Cause if you did, I'm right here."

Kersey kept walking but slowed his pace. He'd let the man catch up. Let him feel confident. His stupidity would grow the longer Kersey waited to respond. Nathan, however, kept looking back.

"Just ignore him, Nathan. Like you said, he's a bad man."

"He a dumb man."

Despite the situation, Kersey laughed. "You got that right, Nathan. He is very dumb."

"Hey, muscle head, you and the tard talking about me? Hey, chicken, I'm talking to you. Maybe you're a tard too."

The hand pushing his back was what he had been waiting for. Kersey whirled with a speed that belied his size. In one smooth motion, he scooped the ignorant fool off the ground by his throat. "Did you have something you wanted to say?"

The man could barely breathe, let alone speak. He struggled to get away. His hands clawed at Kersey's powerful grip. His face morphed through ever deepening shades of red. The driver exited the car and sprinted toward them with a wooden baseball bat. He slowed his approach and wound up with two hands to swing the bat at Kersey.

Kersey pitched the first man into him the second he swung. The driver slowed the swing but could not stop it. A sharp crack similar to a solid hit on a baseball sounded. The first man went down with a shriek. The second man dropped to help his friend. As he did, Kersey ripped the bat away and whipped it at the car. It hit the driver's door with a resounding thud, leaving a dent.

"I'm gonna kill you!" the driver shouted.

"Good luck with that." Kersey grabbed Nathan's hand and led him away.

Over his shoulder, Nathan said, "Yuh. Good luck. He a superhero. Ha."

Kersey passed the house, not wanting the men to see where Nathan lived. Nathan pointed and was about to speak when Kersey pulled him along. "Don't say anything, Nathan. We're going in through the back."

"Okay. Like a secret game?"

"Yes, exactly like that."

They went to the end of the block and turned. Kersey led Nathan to the next block, then cut through the backyard of the house behind Janelle's. He helped Nathan over the fence then hurdled it with one hand on the crossbar. Once inside the house, he checked the front window. The men were up, the driver helping his partner walk. The injured man clutched at his ribs.

He breathed a sigh, then went to get Nathan's after school snack. Peanut butter and Nutella on graham crackers. As the boy munched happily, Kersey sat and watched him eat, thinking this was probably not what Janelle had in mind when she called him.

CHAPTER SEVEN

After his snack, Nathan was ready to play. The schedule called for some form of physical activity, though she specified exercise did not mean calisthenics, weight lifting, long distance running, kickboxing, or any sort of martial arts.

"Let's go outside and play a game."

His peanut butter- and Nutella-covered face beamed a smile. He put two thumbs up and said, "Yuh."

Kersey wiped his face. "You ready?"

"Yuh," then a second later. "No." He held up a hand. "Wait. I do something."

"What?"

"Wait, Ker-sey. I be right back. K?"

"Yeah, sure. Do what you have to."

Nathan hurried up the stairs and disappeared into his room. A series of thumps and bangs came from his room. Kersey was about to go up and see what the commotion was, when he heard, "Aw man!"

Kersey hastened up the stairs and pushed open the door to Nathan's room. He stopped, took in the scene, and stifled a laugh. Nathan had tried to put on the superhero costume, but it was backwards. The cape was draped in the front and Nathan was trying to pull it around to his back.

He noticed Kersey. "Man," he smacked his forehead with an open palm, "I make a mess."

"Yes, you did."

"You help me?"

"Of course." But before he did, he snapped a picture with his phone. "Okay. We have to take it off first. It won't spin around with your arms through the sleeves." Kersey gripped the material and pulled it up until the sleeves were free. He rotated the costume so the cape was in the back before slipping Nathan's arms through the sleeves. "There you go."

"Cool. Thanks, Ker-sey. You my friend."

He struck a pose with hands on hips, chin up, and chest out. The yellow shirt with the big Red S and the word Me underneath was a tight fit, but Nathan didn't care. "Super Me is ready to save the people." He bolted from the room, the red cape fluttering behind.

"Careful on the stairs," Kersey called after him.

Nathan bounded to the bottom, gripped the front door, and yanked it open before Kersey could stop him. He wanted to play in the back to avoid being spotted by the two clowns that confronted them. "Wait, Nathan!" But if Nathan heard, he paid no attention.

By the time Kersey made it to the front porch, Nathan was running around the front yard. His arms were extended in front of him and he swayed side to side like he was flying. The yard sloped toward the street. A sidewalk split the grass with a smaller patch on the curb side.

Nathan stopped at the top of the slope and struck his superhero pose. A young girl of about six years old rode a two-wheel bike past him, stealing a look at him. The glance threw off her balance and the bike dumped on the slope.

In a heartbeat, Nathan was down the slope, helping her up. Kersey stopped his own effort to help to watch Nathan play hero. "You okay?"

Her lip quivered, a prequel to tears, but she managed to control them. "Yes. I think so." Nathan picked up the bike and made a show of examining it, then wiped a few strands of grass from the spokes.

"Ta da. Good as new." He presented it to her like a gift.

She eyed him, too young to be suspicious, but she was certainly curious. "Thank you."

"No problem. That's what superheroes do. Help people."

"Who are you?"

Nathan ran up the slope and hit his pose. "I'm Super Me."

The girl said, "Wow!" She swung a leg over the bike and sat on the seat. "My name's Penny. See you later, Super Me."

"Yuh."

She rode off with Nathan still holding his pose. Once she was out of sight. Kersey said, "Way to go, hero."

"That's what superheroes do." He started down the slope, slipped, and rolled once to the sidewalk. He pushed up on hands and knees. "Oh, man!"

"Come on, Super Me. Let's go in the backyard and see who we can save."

Nathan got to his feet and ran up the driveway, arms out and cape flying. He made a lap around the fenced yard. "Ker-sey, I want to fly. You teach me?"

"Ah, sure." Kersey sized Nathan up and formed a plan. He estimated Nathan weighed about one forty. Not more than he could lift, but not the same as hoisting a barbell. He squatted in front of Nathan, placed his hands on the boy's hips and pushed up. The weight was awkward. Nathan teetered. Kersey needed to find a center of balance. He set Nathan down, repositioned his hands, and tried again. "Okay, now lean forward and stretch out your arms."

It took several attempts for Nathan to understand what to do, but eventually he got it right. Kersey walked backwards, sailing Nathan overhead. Nathan laughed loudly. "Look, Ker-sey. Look at me. I'm flying"

They took a few laps around the yard until Kersey began to tire. He brought Nathan in for a landing. As soon as they touched down, Nathan threw his arms around Kersey's legs. "That was cool."

The sudden impact and Nathan's surprising strength toppled Kersey. He fell on his butt with Nathan landing on top of him. They lay there and laughed hard. Then Nathan pushed to his feet and offered a hand up to Kersey. "Super Me save Ker-sey too."

He assisted the lift and stood. "You're on a roll."

Nathan crinkled up his face, then lifted his feet. He looked at the bottom of each shoe, then held his hands to the sides. No roll. Just grass."

It took a moment for Kersey to make the connection, then he broke out into a loud laugh.

"What?"

"You're a funny boy."

"Not boy. Super Me."

CHAPTER EIGHT

Over the next hour, Kersey found various ways for Nathan to use his super powers and rescue him from increasingly dangerous situations. Kersey checked his phone and saw he was past the allotted time for play. He also noticed he'd missed a text from Janelle. How's it going?

He was in the midst of replying when Nathan said, "Look, Kersey. I fly without you."

"That's good." Then the words registered. "What?" He looked up to see Nathan standing on the wrought iron railing on the porch. He bent his legs and pushed off.

"No!" Kersey dropped the phone and sprinted. He managed to catch Nathan before he face planted but could not prevent his knees and feet from hitting the ground.

The boy went white and burst into a wail. "Owiee! Ow! Ow!" Mommommommom."

"It's okay, Nathan. I've got you."

"Want Mom!" he cried. "Mommommommom."

"She's not here right now. Let me take you inside and look at your legs."

"Noooo! Hurts."

"I know it does. But you're a superhero, and nothing hurts you for long." It was lame, but he didn't know what else to say. He wanted to get him inside, not only to check his injuries, but to get him out of sight from the neighbors. He didn't want one of them to tell Janelle that Nathan had been hurt.

He got him to his feet, but Nathan couldn't take a step. His knees kept folding. Kersey prayed Nathan hadn't broken a leg or displaced a knee cap. He didn't want to take a chance and sat him on the bottom step. He chastised himself for lifting him without first checking the injury. He was messing everything up. He shouldn't have agreed to watch Nathan. He had no experience with kids. What was he thinking?

He rolled up a leg of the black sweat pants that completed the superhero costume. The knee showed a darkening bruise and the shin a scrape. The other knee leg had similar marks. He touched the knee. Nathan winced and pulled back. "Hurts. Don't touch."

"Okay. I think you'll be all right. We need to put ice on the knees and wash the scrapes. Then you'll be back in business."

"No business. Want Mom."

"We'll go inside and get fixed up, and then maybe you can talk to your mom, okay?"

Big drops fell from his eyes, but he was no longer wailing. He wiped at the tears and sniffed and nodded it was all right to go inside. Kersey bent and scooped the boy up. He was forced to set him down to open the door. Kersey walked him into the house and set him at the kitchen table. It took a while to find where Janelle kept the bandages and medical supplies. All the while he searched, Nathan sat with his leg propped up, moaning and staring at the injury.

A small dot of blood welled above the knee. Nathan watched it with wide eyes, then cried out, "Oh!" when it trickled down his leg. Kersey wiped it away. He cleaned the wound and placed a band aid over it, then moved to the shin. The process was repeated twice more to Nathan's winces and ohs.

"There. Good as new."

Nathan didn't look as sure.

"Nathan, you know you can't really fly, right?"

"I can. You saw me."

"Nathan, this is very important." He paused to phrase his words in such a way that Nathan would understand. "You didn't really fly. I was holding you up. We were pretending."

"No." He shook his head. "I can fly."

Kersey tried again. "Well, maybe you can, but sometimes super powers don't work."

"Huh?"

"That's right. Sometimes they don't work. And if you try to fly, you might fall again. It hurt when you fell, didn't it?"

He looked down at the four band aids. "Yuh. Hurts." He winced.

"So you can never fly again unless I'm here to hold you, okay?"

His face crunched together as he thought that through.

"Here's an easy way to remember. "Fly. Hurt." He pointed at the legs. "If you don't want to hurt, don't fly. Never, ever jump off anything. Promise me."

"Okay. I promise. I only fly with Ker-sey."

Kersey sighed. Crisis averted. He'd have to remember to take the band aids off before Janelle got home. "Okay. The schedule says now we do homework."

"Aw man." He slapped a palm to his forehead.

"Come on. How hard can it be? Where's your book bag?"

"I show you."

Nathan sprung from the chair without thought of his injuries. The backpack was on the floor next to the couch. He picked it up and handed it to Kersey. Inside Kersey found a few graded papers and a notebook marked *Homework* on the cover. He flipped to the day's date. *Do flashcards: Numbers 11-20.* That sounded easy enough. He dug through the bag. No flashcards.

"Hey Nathan, did you forget to bring home the flashcards?"

The palm met the forehead again. "Aw man." But there was something different. This time, he peered through his fingers at Kersey, checking his reaction. The eyes twinkled and he fought back a mischievous grin.

"Wait a minute. Did you forget them on purpose?"

He held out his hands to the side and shook his head. "No. I not do that." But his face showed the lie. He covered his mouth with his hands as he burst into laughter.

"Oh, you think you're a wise guy, eh?"

He snorted. "Yuh. Wise guy." He laughed louder.

"You think you fooled me, don't you?"

He pointed at Kersey and laughed some more.

"I got news for you, bub. I can make flashcards."

The laughing stopped. "Make flashcards? What you talking 'bout, Ker-sey? Flashcards at school."

He took a sheet of paper from the notebook, folded it, and tore ten squares. He found a pencil in a pocket on the side of the backpack and wrote the numbers 11-20. "There. Now what do you think, wise guy?"

Nathan looked from Kersey to the freshly made flashcards. "Aw man. You cheat."

"No, I won. I beat you."

"No."

"Let's sit down and work on these."

"No."

"Come on. Superheroes don't skip schoolwork. They have to be smart or they can't help people."

That seemed to convince him. "Once we finish, I'll start making dinner. You can watch TV until it's ready. Deal?"

"Yuh. Deal."

They fist bumped to seal the agreement.

Kersey laid the first square down. The eleven. He figured he'd display them in order first, then mix them up once Nathan had a chance to see each one a few times. "What number is this?"

Before he could answer, someone pounded on the door. "Wait here." He went to the front window and pulled back the curtain. To his dismay, two policemen had come calling.

CHAPTER NINE

Kersey thought, Aw man! and did a mental head slap. Was this about the two guys who assaulted them? He thought about ignoring the knock and pretending they weren't home, but the pounding was more insistent this time and Nathan shouted out, "Who is it?"

Kersey winced, knowing the boy's voice had carried enough to be heard. He had no choice now. He plastered on a happy face and opened the door. Upon seeing his size, both officers stepped back and placed hands on their holstered weapons.

"Good afternoon, officers. Can I assist you with something?"

They tried to see past him into the house. The taller cop, a well-built Hispanic man with Martinez on his name badge, said, "Are you the homeowner?"

"Ah, no. I'm visiting. Is there a problem?"

The black officer was short and round. Cuthbert was on his tag. "Sir, where is the homeowner?"

Both men appeared nervous, which made Kersey edgy. "She's in the hospital. What's this about?"

"Is there a young boy here?" Martinez said.

"Yes."

"We'd like to see him."

"See him?"

"Yes," said Cuthbert. "Is that a problem?"

"No." But clearly there was a problem. "Nathan, can you come here, please?"

No answer. Kersey glanced back. Nathan was not at the dining room table. "Nathan, where are you?" Concerned by his sudden disappearance, Kersey went looking for him. He gave the door a flick but knew the cops would block it and enter. He just wanted a few steps' head start.

He checked the kitchen. Empty. He headed toward the back door.

One of the cops called after him. "Sir, stop right there."

Kersey ignored him. "Nathan. Where are you, buddy?"

The cop's tone became more insistent. "I need you to stop moving now, sir."

Cuthbert shouted, "You will stop or I will be forced to stop you!"

What? What was going on here? He turned in time to catch the twin barbs from the taser in the chest. His body convulsed, stiffened, and toppled. He hit the wall and balanced there like a fallen tree. Martinez ran past, leaping over Kersey's legs as Cuthbert gave him another jolt. He spasmed and slid down the wall.

He felt his arms being twisted behind him and the snap of cuffs. Sometime later, as his mind cleared and feeling returned, he heard, "Found him. He was down the street helping an older lady carry her groceries up the front stairs."

"Why did he leave the house? Was he escaping from the big guy?"

"I asked him that. Says he was working on his flying."

"What's that he's wearing?"

"I guess it's his superhero costume."

"Yuh. I Super Me."

"Well, Super Me, can you tell me who this is?"

Kersey shifted to sit up but his body wouldn't respond yet, so he rolled over instead. He saw Nathan approaching with the two cops. Nathan stopped. "What? Ker-sey." He looked at Martinez. "Why?" He put his arms out to the sides, hands palm up, the way he did when he was confused or didn't know the answer. "He not a bad guy. He superhero, like me."

"So you know this guy?"

"Yuh. He Ker-sey."

Cuthbert squatted in front of him. "Is your name Kersey?"

Anger flared. "Get these cuffs off me."

"Hold on there, big guy. Answer my questions. What's your name?"

Kersey strained against the cuffs, but the effort was futile. He hated being restricted. It took two attempts, but he managed to get to a sitting position. From there he tucked his feet under him and started to stand, but Cuthbert put a hand on his shoulder and shoved him down.

"This will go a lot easier if you answer our questions," Martinez said.

"Don't worry, Ker-sey. I save you." Nathan charged, bowling Cuthbert over. Taken by surprise, the officer fell on top of Kersey with Nathan on top of him. Kersey locked a leg around Cuthbert and rolled, coming out on top and straddling the shocked man. Nathan was laying across the policeman's chest.

Martinez, who had been reaching for Nathan before the impact, stood over the jumble of bodies. Seeing the outcome, he reached for his weapon. Afraid Nathan might get caught in the line of fire, Kersey pushed to his feet and headbutted Martinez in the chest. The force pitched him backward. He tripped over a dining room chair and fell on his back, still fumbling for his gun. As it slid from the holster, Kersey shouted, "No! You might hit Nathan!" then stepped closer and kicked it from the man's hand. A quick look behind showed Cuthbert still trying to get out from under Nathan. This was getting out of hand. He had to defuse the situation before things got worse.

"Okay, let's everyone stay calm and take a step back." Though a fire still burned within him, he backed to a chair and sat. The two cops were on their feet. One held Nathan as the other retrieved his weapon and glared hard at Kersey. Both held guns aimed at him.

"We're taking you in for assaulting a police officer," Martinez said.

"No," Kersey said. He was about to stand, but the pointed barrels made him think better of it. "I have to watch Nathan."

"You should have thought about that before you attacked us."

"And I suppose I attacked you before you tazed me?" That gave them pause. "You had no cause to do that when all I was doing was searching for a missing boy. That'll look good on someone's report."

"We feared for the boy's safety. Besides, it'll be our word against yours."

"Will it? It might go that way at the beginning, but how will it end once I involve lawyers?"

Cuthbert holstered his weapon. "Let's try this again. What's your name?"

"Kersey."

"Kersey what?"

"Mitchell."

Before he could go any further, a phone rang. Kersey followed the tone and realized it was his. He had placed it on the dining room table when they started doing the flashcards. Martinez looked at it then picked it up.

"Who's Janelle?"

Kersey's heart sank. "It's Nathan's mother. Uncuff me and let me answer so she doesn't think there's a problem with Nathan."

Martinez got a glint in his eye and answered. "Hello." He listened. "This is Officer Yuriel Martinez, ma'am." Janelle's voice came through the speaker loud enough to be heard. "Yes, I have your son. He's fine." Pause. "He is the problem. Can you identify and describe the man, please?" He listened longer. "Thank you, ma'am. Of course. We were responding to a call from one of your neighbors who claimed a strange man was beating up your son. Evidently, Nathan was crying. The neighbor heard but did not recognize the man. When we got here, this Kersey refused to answer questions. When he couldn't find your son, we took action." Pause. "Yes, we found him down the street and brought him home." More listening. Kersey hung his head. Less than three hours and he'd already failed.

"Of course, you can speak with him."

Kersey lifted his head with renewed hope. He'd at least get the chance to explain. Martinez walked past him and handed the phone to Nathan. "Your mother wishes to speak with you."

"Mommy." He took the phone with exuberance. "Hi Mommy. When you come home?" He listened for a moment, giving a few uh-huhs, then said, "We being superheroes. We save a girl and her bike. Kersey teach me to fly. I fall. Hurts. Yuh. Then the police came and we fight them." Pause. "Huh?" Pause. "Yuh. Fun."

Martinez smirked. Kersey felt the heat rise on his face.

"Yuh. Okay. Bye, Mommy. Love you too." He handed the phone to Martinez, then came over and sat on Kersey's lap. Whatever she was saying to Martinez had the man smiling. Nathan grabbed Kersey's cheeks and gazed into his eyes. "Mommy's mad at you. You in big tro-uble." He drew out the word to emphasize the point.

"Yes, ma'am. Now that we know what's going on, we'll take care of it. You rest and recuperate. I'm sure things will settle down here. Right. Goodbye."

He set the phone down. "Guess we won't need to take you in after all. I think you're in enough trouble without us."

Cuthbert uncuffed Kersey and the two men walked out laughing.

CHAPTER TEN

That Janelle didn't want to speak to him was all Kersey needed to verify Martinez's statement.

"That was fun. We good superheroes."

"Yeah. Great."

"Being a superhero is hard work. I hungry now. Feed me, Kersey."

"Yeah, I'll get right on that." The food schedule called for spaghetti. Fortunately, that was one of the few things he knew how to make. Janelle made it easier by having a store bought sauce that Nathan liked.

While he waited for the spaghetti water to boil, Kersey tried to think of what to say to Janelle. She was mad and he couldn't blame her, but in truth, it wasn't his fault. Not that it was an excuse when it came to her son, but he hated that she was mad at him. She'd never trust him with Nathan again.

He walked to the doorway to check on Nathan. He didn't trust that he'd stay put after he left the house earlier. He was watching a cartoon about talking dogs that morphed into...what else? Superheroes.

"Hey, Nathan."

"Yuh," he said without taking his eyes from the screen.

"You should probably take off the costume."

"No." It came out as a pained whine.

"You don't want to get spaghetti sauce on it. It'll stain, then you won't be able to wear it anymore."

His lip quivered.

"It's up to you, but you should change. You can put it on again after dinner, okay?"

"K." He refocused on the TV.

Kersey drained the noodles, placed a pile on a plate, and topped it with sauce. Then he carried the plates out to the dining room table. "Time to eat, Nathan. Oh. Forgot the silverware." He ducked back into the kitchen and grabbed forks and knives and set them on the table. He scanned the surface to see if he forgot anything else. "Drinks. "What do you want to drink, ah, Nathan?" The boy was no longer in front of the TV.

Though a spike of panic pierced him, he remained calm. He'd told Nathan to change his outfit. He hurried to the stairs and called up. "Nathan? Dinner's ready." No reply. No sound. Now he was worried. As he started up the stairs, he shot a glance toward the front door. His heart dropped like an anchor into water. The door was open a crack.

He jumped down the stairs, ripped the door open, and ran out onto the porch. He was about to shout his name but thought better of it. He didn't need the neighborhood to know he'd lost Nathan again. He scanned the area from the top step but saw no flying red cape or flash of yellow. Nothing. Panic gripped him like a vise.

He leaped down the four stairs and broke into a jog as soon as his feet touched down. Left or right? He chose right and picked up speed. How long had Nathan been gone? How far could he go? Had he been that upset about changing out of his costume that he'd run away? Dear God, Janelle was going to kill him.

His phone vibrated. It was Janelle. His heart sank to the ground. He debated whether to answer. If he did, she'd be mad, but if he didn't, she'd worry. Worrying was worse. He stopped running to control his breathing but kept walking as he accepted the call.

"Hey, Janelle. How are you doing?"

Silence. "Where's Nathan?" Her voice was calm, but her tone was icy.

"I'm looking for him now."

"What do you mean *looking for*?"

"Oh, sorry. Didn't mean to worry you. We're playing hide and seek."

"Did you lose my son again?"

"What? No. Of course not." A flash of yellow darted across his sight line. "In fact, I just found his hiding spot." Kersey hurried to catch the boy. He rounded the corner and found him posing for a group of younger kids.

"I want to speak to him."

"Ah, sure. Let me get him."

"Put my son on the phone now!" All calm and pretense of such was gone.

"Okay. He's right here."

Nathan was fielding questions from the group that was made up of five-or six-year-olds. One little girl with pigtails spoke with awe. "You mean you are a real superhero?"

"Yuh"

"Nathan!" Kersey called. "I found you," he continued, trying to sell the hide and seek story. Nathan looked like he was about to run. "It's your mom. She's on the phone."

"Mommy?"

"Yeah. She wants to talk to you." He closed the distance in a hurry, arm extended with the phone. As Nathan took it, Kersey clamped a hand around his arm and led him down the street. He tried to hear the conversation, but all he caught was Nathan saying yuh several times to whatever Janelle was asking.

"K. Bye, Mommy. Love you too."

He handed the phone to Kersey. It was bad that she still didn't want to speak with him. As he took it, Nathan gave his arm a twist and broke free. He started running. Taken by surprise, Kersey pursued. Had Nathan just distracted him to break away? The boy was devious.

Kersey caught him in four strides. He jogged alongside, not wanting to touch Nathan for fear of knocking him off stride. If he tripped and fell, getting him to settle down would be a nightmare.

Nathan turned his red face toward him and smiled. Evidently, he thought this was funny. At least he was heading toward home.

Across the street, a car door slammed. A loud voice yelled, "Get back here!"

Kersey glanced and saw a young woman walking fast toward a house. A man in a parked car shouted at her through the open passenger window. As he watched, the man exited, slamming his door and following. "Don't you walk away from me. I'm warning you."

The woman pivoted, face enraged, and shouted back, "Or what? What will you do?"

"Don't test me."

"Oh, big man. You gonna hit me again?" That stopped him for the moment. "We're done. I don't ever wanna see you again. I'm not taking your abuse anymore." She whirled and walked away, but he wasn't done with her. He grabbed her arm, yanked her back, and slapped her face. The smack echoed across the street. She put a hand to her cheek, shock on her face.

"Get back in the car now!" he ordered.

Kersey stopped. He shouldn't get involved, especially not with Nathan present. Nathan! He stopped, realizing the boy was no longer next to him. He cursed under his breath and spun around. Where had he gone?

Then the nightmare continued as he heard, "Super Me to the rescue!"

Kersey turned back to the warring couple and spied Nathan, cape flapping behind him, running straight at the man. He hit him from behind; whether intentional or not, Kersey couldn't say. Both the man and Nathan looked surprised by the contact. They went down in a heap and rolled. Kersey bolted across the street without looking and almost got taken out by a Prius.

He reached the other side in time to see the man roll on top of Nathan. He drew back his fist to punch Nathan in the face. Kersey could barely breathe, seeing he would not be in time to stop the damage. However, the young woman leaped on the man's back and pummeled him, flailing wildly.

He reached back, grabbed her hair and yanked her off, then kicked her away. That gave Nathan the chance to act. He brought his knee up to stand, but it made contact with the man's groin instead. The man howled and lowered his hands to protect himself from a second blow.

Nathan scrambled out from under the man, but he recovered in time to snag Nathan's cape. He pulled backward and Nathan fell. As the man moved to land a punch, Kersey stepped up with fist already cocked and let it fly. The man's face seemed to crumble in on itself. He fell back, landed with a thud, and did not move.

Kersey feared he'd killed him. He scooped Nathan up and checked him over. The boy came up smiling. "That was cool."

Kersey frowned. It was anything but cool.

The woman crawled to the fallen man and checked his pulse. "He still has a heartbeat and he's still breathing."

Kersey feared she would turn on him but instead, she said, "Can you hit him again?"

CHAPTER ELEVEN

Back in the house, Kersey closed and locked the door, then peeked out the window in case the police had been called. That would be all he needed—the cops at Janelle's house twice in one day.

Nathan buzzed around the house. He was pumped full of adrenaline and not interested in the now cold spaghetti. Kersey corralled him. "Nathan, you can't leave the house without me knowing. You understand that?"

Nathan made no reply.

"If you did that to your mom, she'd be mad, wouldn't she?"

"Yuh."

"Then you can't do it to me, either. Okay?"

Still no reply.

"Nathan, if you don't answer me, I'm going to have to tell your mom you went outside without asking. You want me to do that?"

"No. Don't tell Mommy."

"Then promise me you won't run away again."

He thought about it, put his hand behind his back, and said, "Promise." With the other hand he crossed his heart.

"Nathan, are your fingers crossed behind your back?"

His face reddened. He shrugged.

"You don't know if they're crossed?"

"They not crossed." He brought both hands out and showed them palms up. "Not now."

"Yeah, that's what I thought. Are you ready to eat?"

"I save the girl. You see me? I superhero!" His arms went up and he held the word a few seconds.

"Yes, you are. But superheroes have to eat after they save people. Otherwise, they lose their strength and can't save people anymore."

He pondered. "Okay. Let's eat. Get strong and save more girls."

"Good boy. Now, sit at the table and I'll heat up the food."

Kersey didn't bother trying to get him to change out of his costume. No sense making him upset and risking another run. He covered him with a kitchen towel and two napkins and hoped for the best. Nathan ate with gusto and kept a constant monologue about his heroic exploits. Nathan's exuberance slopped the sauce all over himself and the table.

Kersey wiped Nathan's face with a damp towel and had him help clear the table. He decided to do the dishes after Nathan was asleep, afraid if he turned his back the boy would run again. They watched TV for a while until it was time for bed.

They went upstairs. Kersey went down the checklist Janelle left him to make sure everything was done. Brush teeth, wash face and hands, dirty clothes in hamper, change into Spiderman pajamas, say prayers, and read a story.

Kersey sat on the edge of the bed. "What story do you want me to read?" Two shelves had been dedicated to Nathan's library. He scanned down the row, reading titles.

"No book, Ker-sey. You tell me a story."

"You want me to make one up?"

"Yuh."

He was stymied. "I, uh, I don't think I know any stories."

"Yuh, Ker-sey does. You superhero too, like me. Tell a superhero story."

"Ah, okay." His mind raced to latch onto a storyline. He chose one of his own missions but substituted a young boy for himself and cut out most of the gruesome details.

"Once upon a time, there was a young boy who had super powers."

"He fly?"

"Yeah, sure. He could fly."

"Cool."

"The boy flew over the town looking for anyone who needed help. One day he spotted a man trying to kidnap—er, dognap a little puppy. This super flying boy flew down and landed next to the man. 'You can't steal that puppy,' the superhero boy said." Kersey altered his voice for the character. Nathan giggled.

"'Why not?' asked the thief." He changed voices again. "The superhero replied, 'Because it doesn't belong to you. Think about how sad the family will be if they lose their puppy.' The thief thought that over. He didn't want to make anyone sad. 'But I want a puppy.' 'Then let's go get one who needs a friend.' The thief put the puppy down and the superhero helped him find one of his own. Then everyone lived happily ever after. The end."

"Yay."

"Okay. Time for sleep."

"Ker-sey. You be here tomorrow?"

"Yes. For a while. But your mom is coming home tomorrow, so you'll get to see her."

"Ker-sey. You stay here. Live with Mommy and me. We be superheroes together."

Kersey smiled. Wonder what Janelle would think of that idea? "Goodnight, Nathan."

"Night, Ker-sey."

He got up, made sure the nightlight was on, then pulled the door closed enough for the bathroom light to filter through. He stood in the hall for a moment, relishing the quiet. It had been quite the adventurous day.

As he went downstairs, he realized that despite the extra events not on Janelle's list and of course, her anger at him, he had fun.

CHAPTER TWELVE

After finishing the dishes, Kersey wiped down the kitchen counters and the table. The effort wasn't so much to clean up or feel domestic as much as to score points with Janelle in hopes of offsetting his failures. He checked his phone. No texts or missed calls from Janelle or Aleeyah. He felt hollow.

He sat back on the couch and propped his feet on the coffee table. An instant later, he whipped them down as if they were on fire. He was sure Janelle would not be happy if she walked in and saw him with his feet on the furniture. He thought about it for a moment, then took off his shoes and put his feet back up. That was better.

He thought about sending a message to Aleeyah, but what would he say? He could apologize again, but if the first twenty times hadn't worked, what good would the twenty-first be? In his line of work, people came together and drifted apart often. It was accepted as the norm. He hated that it ended with her being upset with him. Sure it had almost cost her life, but—but what? There was no but for that. He had almost gotten her killed. That was inexcusable. He'd have walked away too if the roles were reversed. Even had she stayed she'd never be the same. There would always be that doubt in her mind that he might not show up. No, he screwed up. Their partnership was over and he had no one else to blame but himself.

He moved on. He should send a message to Janelle to at least let her know Nathan was safe and sleeping. A sudden thought hit him. He hurried up the stairs, crept to Nathan's door and peeked in. For a moment, he was afraid the boy had slipped out without him noticing, but the glow of the nightlight lit his round, now angelic face.

Downstairs, he sat and composed a message to Janelle. He started over several times before settling on *All's well. Nathan sleeping. Hope you are doing well.* He paused, rereading it three times. What else should he say? What else could he say? He pressed send.

He put his feet up and clicked on the TV. As he scrolled down the channels, he heard a vehicle pull up and park in front of the house. Distant voices filtered through the wall, but not loud enough to be understood. A minute later there was a knock on the door. Startled, he sat up and checked the time. It was a little after nine. The knock came again, but louder. He didn't want to wake Nathan, so he stood to intercept the next knock.

He reached the door and peered through the window at the top. A young woman stood there dressed in nice slacks and a beige top. She brushed a strand of hair back and wet her lips, ready to speak as soon as the door swung open. For a moment, an image of the mother from the school flitted past his eyes, but when she turned, he was sure it wasn't her.

He wondered if she was selling something, but it was rather late for a solicitor. He hoped she would go away, but even as he dismissed the notion, she raised a slim arm to rap again. He unlocked the door and opened it a crack.

"What?"

"Hi. I'm Rose Pantera with WLRQ TV. Are you the young superhero's father?"

A frigid blast iced the blood in his veins. Oh, no. Not a reporter.

"One of our viewers sent a video of a young boy rushing to the aid of a woman who was being accosted. I'm here to interview him."

"You have the wrong house. Go away." He closed the door.

It had been closed for less than two seconds before she knocked again.

Kersey opened the door wider. His anger must have been apparent on his face as she paled and backed a step. "If you knock again, I will call the police. Now leave us alone." Kersey was going to try to intimidate her to leave when he noticed a cameraman on the sidewalk. He had the camera up and appeared to be filming.

Regaining her composure, Rose Pantera stepped closer and thrust a microphone in his face. "Is this the house of the young superhero who saved the woman earlier in the day? Our viewers would like the meet him."

"I'm telling you once more, you have the wrong house. My kids are asleep. They have school tomorrow. If you wake them, I will call the police. We have nothing more to say."

She lowered the mic and leaned closer. Her voice was low but intense. "Well, sir, you can either talk to me now or I will camp outside your door and speak to the young man tomorrow." She gave him a defiant look.

Kersey felt his anger boil. He lifted his cell phone and pretended to punch in 911. He waited a second and said, "I'd like to report a woman on my porch harassing me. I have asked her several times to leave, but she refuses. She says she's a reporter, but I think she's a stalker.

"Yes, she looks to be about sixteen. White. Dressed in brown slacks and a beige blouse. She's holding what looks like one of those karaoke microphones." He lowered his voice and cupped a hand around the phone, but said loud enough to be heard, "I think she's on drugs." Rose's mouth gaped and her face darkened. "No, ma'am. I won't let her inside. I'm trying to protect my children. Who knows what she might be capable of? You can never be too safe these days."

Her eyes narrowed. Her body hunched, ready to spring.

"Have a nice night," he said and closed the door.

Before it shut, she said, "You're going to be sorry you messed with me."

Kersey said into the phone, "Officer, she just threatened me."

He stood by the door and waited. She stomped her feet on the porch in a tantrum. He risked a peek. She clomped down the steps. Kersey hoped he'd won and she would go away. His elation high, he was about to turn away when he noticed the cameraman point up. The reporter whirled around, looked where he pointed, and beamed brightly. Kersey glanced up as well but could not see what they spotted. Rose Pantera lowered her gaze, caught Kersey's through the window, and gave him a triumphant smirk.

Uh-oh, that can't be good. Kersey turned and ran up the stairs. He crept to Nathan's room and peered in. To his shock and dismay, Nathan stood on his dresser, highlighted in the window. He was dressed in his costume and in his superhero pose for all the world, including Rose Pantera, to see.

Janelle was going to kill him, resuscitate him, and kill him again.

CHAPTER THIRTEEN

"Nathan," Kersey said, his voice louder than intended. "Get down from there."

"The people come to see me. I superhero."

"Yes, but don't you know the rules of being a superhero?"

He did a doubletake. "Rules? What rules?"

"When you're a superhero, you're not supposed to let people know who you really are. You have to hide your secret identity."

"Hide your 'dentity? But how the people know I superhero?"

"They're not supposed to. That's why it's a secret. Otherwise, the bad guys know where you live. You don't want that. If the bad guys know where to find you, they'll be after you all the time. That's not good. You're supposed to chase them. They're not supposed to chase you."

"Oh."

"Yeah. You better get down. That lady out there is a reporter. She's the worst kind of bad guy. She'll tell everyone where the bad guys can find you." He crossed the room and lifted Nathan down. "And didn't I put those clothes in the laundry hamper?"

"Yuh. They not dirty, Ker-sey. They superhero clothes. They not get dirty."

"Oh. I didn't know that. But they do get wrinkled, and if you wear them to bed they will be too wrinkled to wear tomorrow after school."

Kersey helped him get dressed in his pajamas again and into bed. In the hall he moved to the window. Rose Pantera was standing next to the driver's side door while her cameraman loaded his equipment in the back. She glanced up, spotted him, and smiled broadly. She gave a victory wave and climbed into the van. Kersey watched as they drove away, wondering how much more trouble she'd cause him. With any luck, the film she captured of Nathan would not make it to the eleven o'clock news in time to be aired. If his luck was really holding, Janelle would never see it when it did air.

As his father used to say, there's good luck, bad luck, and no luck. The odds were against him. He hung his head and walked down the steps.

Time took an eternity to reach eleven o'clock. When the news came on, he moved to the edge of the sofa and watched with growing anxiety. With each passing story, he began to relax. As the weather report aired, his confidence expanded. Next up would be sports, then a few closing stories, and...

His phone dinged from an incoming text. It was from Janelle. If his worry returned knowing she was still awake, the message made him cringe. *You'd better keep my son safe or I swear I will hunt you down.*

Kersey had faced down a lot of bad people and never had the same all-encompassing fear the message conveyed. He read it again, but it didn't get any better. He messaged back *Understood,* then pushed back into the plush sofa cushions as if seeking protection.

The sports ended and they went to commercial. Kersey checked his watch and blew out a long breath. There could only be time for one more story. He looked at his hand, realizing he had crossed his fingers unconsciously.

The news came back on. The smiling female anchor said, "And just when you think there is only darkness left, a bright shining light appears to give us hope. Rose?"

At the sound of her name, Kersey sat up straight, his heart seizing up. "That's right, Evelyn. This was sent in by one of our viewers. It's a young boy dressed in what looks like a homemade superhero costume rushing to the rescue of a young woman being physically abused by a man."

"Oh no!" Kersey slapped his hands to his face, splaying his fingers to watch the impending train wreck.

"The young as-yet unidentified boy tackles the assailant, ignoring the risks of injury to himself."

The video cut before Kersey entered the fray. "Thank God for small blessings." Then the picture switched to the house and Kersey shrunk lower into the cushion. "I tried to interview the young man but was told he was asleep. However, we did manage to catch this image from a bedroom window."

There stood Nathan, posed in the window in costume for all the world to see.

"Evelyn, I think the world may yet be saved."

"What an incredible and heartwarming story, Rose. I hope you will follow up on the further exploits of our city's savior."

Rose Pantera's image grew on the screen as the camera closed in on her. "You can count on it." Her eyes appeared to bore straight into his soul. The message had been delivered. She was not done with him yet. His only hope now was that Janelle had not seen the story.

At that moment, his phone dinged again with an incoming text and his last thread of hope was ripped from him. He didn't want to look but had no choice. *Run. Hide. You're dead.*

Whatever last chance he might have held onto crumbled around him. He messaged back as fast as his fingers would move. *I'm sorry. I can explain. I was right there. It wasn't as bad as the reporter made it look.*

Don't care.

And with that, his fate was sealed. Janelle would never allow him within a mile of Nathan, let alone near her. He shut down the TV, curled up on the sofa, and stared at the ceiling.

CHAPTER FOURTEEN

Having barely slept, Kersey went through the motions of getting Nathan fed and dressed for school. For his part, the sleepy faced boy was in good spirits. He came downstairs wearing the costume, having dug it out of the hamper again. That was all he needed; to have Janelle's first sighting of her son be in that costume.

He had to approach the situation carefully to prevent Nathan from making a scene. "Nathan," he whispered. "Remember what I told you yesterday about keeping your superhero persona a secret?"

"Yuh."

"You can't wear the outfit to school."

"Aw man."

"Sorry, Super Me. You don't want everyone to know who you are, or the bad guys will find you. You don't want them to hurt your friends, do you?"

"No." He hung his head low and stared into his cereal bowl. His lower lip stuck out and quivered.

"Besides, I think the school has a rule about no superhero costumes. You understand that, don't you?"

Nathan nodded and wiped at a tear. "You're a good boy, Nathan. And a good superhero. Come on. I'll help you change." Kersey held out a hand. He thought Nathan would rebel against the change, but he surprised Kersey by taking his hand.

After breakfast, Kersey opened the door to walk Nathan to school. True to her word, Rose Pantera and her cameraman stood outside next to a station van. At seeing the door open, she became animated, talking to the cameraman and hastening toward the house.

Kersey slammed the door shut. His mind whirled, searching for an escape plan. "Hey, Nathan, how about if we play a game and go to school a secret way?"

Whether from the excitement in Kersey's voice, the mention of the word secret, or just because they were doing something different, Nathan's face lit and his head bobbed. "Yuh. But Ker-sey, what we gonna do?" He put his palm up.

"We're gonna go out the back and hop the fence."

Nathan looked skeptical.

"Oh come on, superhero. You may not be able to dress in your costume, but you can still act like a hero. Where's your spirit of adventure? Come on. Let's try."

"K."

Kersey took Nathan's hand and led him to the back door. He glanced in both directions. So far, it was clear. "We have to be very quiet. It's more fun if we can sneak out without anyone knowing we're gone."

The glow returned to Nathan's face, erasing his doubts. They stepped out and Kersey closed the door soundlessly. They crept across the yard toward the back fence. Kersey gripped Nathan by the hips and hoisted. He leaned over the four-foot high fence, Nathan squealing with the lift. He set him down, but Nathan had a death grip around his neck and didn't let go until sure he was on solid footing. Kersey placed a hand on the crossbar and hurdled the fence in one quick sweep of his legs.

"Wow!" Nathan exclaimed. "That was cool. Teach me, Ker-sey."

"Shh! Later. We have to be quiet and hurry or we'll be late for school." He took Nathan's hand and moved before he was ready, almost pulling him to the ground. Once moving, Kersey increased speed until they were down the neighbor's driveway and on the sidewalk.

He scanned for any sight of Rose Pantera. To his relief, she had not caught on to the deception. They reached the school with five minutes to spare and no one in pursuit. The teacher met them at the door. The rest of the class was already standing in a straightish line.

As they approached, Kersey heard a boy say, "Hey! There's that superhero kid." He pointed and the others around him looked. The recognition annoyed Kersey. The kid should've been in bed at that time. Where were his parents? Fortunately, Nathan did not hear him.

"Good morning, Nathan," Mrs. Wilson said. "Guess you had a busy day yesterday." Though the words were directed toward Nathan, her gaze was aimed at Kersey. She obviously disapproved of Nathan's extracurricular activities.

"Ah, it wasn't what it seemed," Kersey said, hoping to defuse the coming inquisition.

"Do tell."

"Ah, maybe another time."

She nodded sagely as if that would be better. "Tell me, Mr. Kersey, will you be picking Nathan up after school?"

"I don't think so. I believe his mother will be here."

"Well, too bad. I would've liked to hear this story. Well, I'm sure Nathan's mother will be glad to get things back to normal—for Nathan's sake." The meaning was clear. He had caused enough disruption in Nathan's life. He sighed.

"No doubt." He dropped to one knee. "Have a good day, Nathan." He didn't want to say goodbye here, in case it upset Nathan.

"Yuh."

To his surprise, Nathan wrapped his arms around Kersey's neck and hugged him. Kersey couldn't help but think he already knew this was their goodbye. He stood, smiled at him, and backed away. Nathan waved, his face scrunching up in his trademark smile. Kersey waved back, then turned as he felt his eyes fill.

Behind him he heard Nathan tell a classmate. "That's Ker-sey. My friend. He a Super Me, too."

The tear fell, rolling on a leisurely path down his face. He did not wipe at it. Instead, he let it run its course. He wanted to remember the feeling the next time he thought about Nathan.

CHAPTER FIFTEEN

Kersey walked back to the house, forgetting that Rose Pantera would most likely still be standing outside. Four houses from Janelle's she came storming toward him, arms swinging like a speed walker and the microphone twirling like a baton. She had a definite purpose to her advance. Either physical or verbal harm for Kersey.

She planted her feet in front of him, hands on hips and fire in her eyes. "You think you've won, don't you?"

Before she could begin her rant, Kersey said, "Yes," and stepped around her.

"Hey! I'm talking to you."

"No, you're not."

"Yes, I am."

"No, you're yelling at me."

"So?"

"So, I don't have to listen. Have a nice day." He turned in front of her and headed up Janelle's driveway. Rose Pantera followed.

"You haven't seen the last of me. I'm going to get my story, and you can't stop me. It will be much more favorable for you if you cooperate, though."

"That sounds like a threat, Ms. Pantera." He spun around fast. Unable to stop her progress, she bumped face first against his chest. She emitted a squeak and put her hands up to push off, then hesitated and let her hand drag across the broad span of muscle. Her lips pursed into an O.

"Are you assaulting me now?" he asked.

"What? No. Of course not. I, ah…" Her face flushed.

"Nice rosy color," he said.

A hand lifted to her cheek. The color darkened from an embarrassed shade to a stormy red. "Listen here, bub…"

"Name's not bub. Have a good day." He stepped into the backyard, inserted the key in the door and closed it, leaving her sputtering.

Once behind the safety of the door, Kersey released a breath, thankful he wouldn't have to deal with her anymore.

He spent the better part of an hour going cleaning, wiping, and picking up. It was important to him things were in perfect condition when Janelle came home. He might have failed in other areas, but the few brownie points he might garner from the clean house couldn't hurt.

Finished, he glanced out the front window. Rose and her cameraman were gone, but he felt confident they'd be back and didn't doubt for a moment they'd be waiting at the school for Nathan's dismissal. Janelle, fresh out of surgery, would be forced to deal with her. Maybe he should stick around to serve as bodyguard.

He decided to stay until he heard from Janelle, in case there was a problem with her release. He didn't want to leave Nathan stranded at school.

Staking out a job, doing recon, or waiting to put a plan in motion took a special skill. To stay motionless for long periods of time was not easy, but Kersey was good at it. However, sitting around idly with no purpose other than watching time pass made him antsy. He got up several times and walked to the kitchen or the front windows. When neither offered any distraction from the tedium, he paced from the front room through the dining room and down the hall and back.

What felt like an entire day turned out to be less than forty minutes. He flopped on the sofa, clicked on the TV, and scrolled through the channels. Then he left it on a cooking show for the noise.

Kersey slid his cell phone from his pocket and scanned messages. None. He thought about sending a text to Janelle, then decided against it. It was still early. The doctor most likely wouldn't be doing rounds until later. He had offered to pick her up from the hospital, but she refused, saying she had already set up transportation with the hospital's shuttle service. His thoughts drifted to Aleeyah. He desperately wanted to reach out to her but didn't know what to say.

He typed in a message, erased it, tried again, and erased that. He sat back, frustrated and annoyed with his own inadequacies. Then he sat up and typed in, *I'm sorry. Please reach out.* He paused over the send button, then pressed down. The text was sent. He sat back, relieved. Hopefully she had reconsidered and was willing to forgive him.

Seconds later, the phone dinged with an incoming text. Excited, he looked at the screen. *Unable to connect. Phone no longer in service.* His excitement burst like a bubble. Aleeyah really was serious about never working together again. She had dumped her phone. That meant she was long gone.

Kersey wondered if she'd taken another job somewhere. A sadder thought was that she had taken another partner. The sofa sucked him down deeper into the cushions and his own depression. He sat there for close to an hour before the phone rang.

A quick uninterest glance showed it was Janelle. That perked him up.

"Hello?"

"Kersey?"

"Yes. It's me."

"Are you still in the city?"

"Yeah. I'm at the house right now. Did you want me to leave?"

"No. Actually, the opposite. I'm not being released until two or three, depending on when the doctor gets here. I may not be able to get to the school in time to pick up Nathan. Would you mind?"

"No, of course not. I'd be happy to." The words rushed from his mouth, tumbling over each other. He rolled his eyes and slapped his forehead to get himself to slow down and take a breath.

"That's not going to interfere with any plans?"

"No, not at all."

'That's great. I, uh, appreciate this."

He had the feeling she wanted to say something else but was being polite, like and try not to get my son hurt.

"I'll pick him up and stay until you arrive." His mind raced for something to say. "Are you doing all right?"

"Yes. Fine. Thank you."

Silence weighed heavy.

"I should go. The nurse just walked in. I'll call if I get out earlier."

"Okay. Good. Take care." Take care? "Bye." But she had already hung up. "Ugh!" He was acting like a high school boy on his first date. Well, at least he was going to see her before he left. That was a good thing, wasn't it?

He thought about the mess he'd made of his babysitting duties. Maybe it wasn't such a good thing after all.

CHAPTER SIXTEEN

At two-thirty, Kersey peeked out the front window. Rose Pantera and her cameraman were nowhere in sight. That was good and bad. Good, because her absence would make the short walk to school much less stressful; but bad, because she might be waiting to ambush him.

He left the house and closed and locked the door, then jogged down the steps and down the block to get distance from the house, should she make an appearance. He slowed his pace in the next block, still arriving a half hour early.

He leaned against the fence and checked his phone. No new messages from Janelle. His thoughts jumped to what he would do once Janelle came home and no longer needed or wanted him around. He could drive back to the Kansas City area and try to track down Aleeyah, but she was a pro. If she didn't want to be found, he'd never find her.

He might just drive with no destination in mind. Eventually, someone would have need of his services. He didn't need to take on any more jobs. He had enough money to live frugally for the next twenty years. But if he did nothing, his well-honed skills would become rusty and his body would begin to sag. No, he'd look for some kind of work until he no longer functioned at such a high level.

"Well hello there, big man."

The voice startled him. He turned to see Martha approaching and wearing a smile that would embarrass the Cheshire Cat. Her hand snaked toward his bicep and clamped down, the nails sinking deep. Kersey winced at the touch like he'd been bitten by an asp.

"Still jumpy, I see. That's all right. I like a man who jumps."

"I, uh…"

"And such a conversationalist too. Don't worry, hon. I'll talk for both of us."

Kersey didn't doubt that for a second.

"I didn't get your name last time."

"It's, ah…" He forgot it as Martha trailed her nails down his spine.

"Ah? That's an interesting name."

"It's Kersey." Did his voice just squeak?

"Kersey." She said it like it was the answer to an important question. "Kerrrrsey." She rolled the r and repeated it several more times, dragging out the r longer and more annoyingly each time.

"So Kerrrrsey, what do you do for fun?"

He wanted to answer, "Not this," or even better, "I do severe harm to those who need pain." What came out instead was, "I'm a fitness trainer."

"Oh! How perfect is that? I need a personal trainer."

Behind her, Kersey spotted a van with WLRQ painted in bright red letters. Just what he needed. It kept moving out of sight. They were either going to park and walk back to the school or trap him somewhere on the street.

The dismissal bell rang. Kersey gave a quick smile to Martha and stepped around her. He moved toward the door, then realized his mistake when the doors burst open and an endless stream of anxious kids were vomited from the building. Tiny bodies swarmed around and past him.

Minutes later, Mrs. Wilson's very orderly class walked out in one straight line. Nathan was third from the back. Mrs. Wilson lifted an inquisitive eyebrow upon seeing him. Kersey smiled and said,

"Doctor hasn't released her yet. She was afraid she wouldn't get here in time to pick Nathan up, so she asked if I'd do it."

"That presents a problem. We weren't informed that you would be picking him up."

Kersey understood. "You can call her if you need to verify."

"That would be a good idea. I'm sorry, but I take my responsibility for the safety of the children seriously."

"I respect that."

She patted her pockets, Kersey guessed searching for her cell phone.

"Here, use mine. Her number is the first one in the call list." She took it, thanked him, and stepped away to call.

Nathan ran up and wrapped his arms around Kersey. "Ker-sey. You still here."

"Yep. Still here."

Then a look of confusion crossed his face. "Where's Mommy?"

"She's coming. We'll meet her at home."

"Cool. You stay too?"

"I'm not sure yet. I may have to go to work."

"What work? You superhero."

"Yeah, but I still need to pay the bills."

Mrs. Wilson returned and handed Kersey the phone. "All set. She's getting ready to leave the hospital now. Thank you for being understanding."

"Not a problem. For what it's worth, you do an exceptional job with these kids."

She beamed. "Thank you."

Kersey took Nathan's hand and froze. Rose Pantera stood at the corner with her trusty cameraman in tow.

"Nathan, let's play the game where we sneak around the block."

"Yuh." His face lit like a hundred watt bulb.

Kersey led him away from the corner, ducking low and trying to keep others between him and Rose. The longer he could put off discovery, the better the chances of reaching the house without confrontation.

They reached the street and ducked behind parked cars waiting to cross. Rose spotted them and shouted and pointed. To Kersey's surprise, she took off at a full sprint. He hadn't expected that. She must really want this story, he thought, yanking Nathan's arm for him to move faster.

They lost sight of her as they went past the corner house. Kersey tried to estimate how much time they'd have before she rounded the corner, and it wasn't as long as he hoped. They hadn't gotten halfway down the first block before Rose rounded the corner at a long-legged steady pace.

As she closed, he heard, "I ran track in college. You don't stand a chance of outrunning me."

Kersey took her at her word and began planning. They reached the first corner and turned left. Rose was less than thirty yards behind and closing fast. He was going to have to intercept her, which meant sending Nathan on ahead. He would not have been able to climb the fence by himself, so Kersey opted to come in from the front.

He fished the house key from his pocket. Nathan was breathing hard. He wasn't going to make it much farther. Kersey slowed. "Nathan, I don't want to scare you, but there's a bad lady following us."

Alarm sprang to his face. "Bad lady? He tried to look over his shoulder, but that only slowed them more.

"Nathan, listen to me. Do you know how to unlock the front door?"

"Unlock? Yuh."

"So if I give you the key and tell you to run, you can get inside?"

"Yuh." His breath was ragged.

Kesey risked a peek. Rose was no more than fifteen yards away. The corner of the short block was in front of them. He wanted to make the turn so Nathan had a straight two block route. Kersey would run interference until Nathan disappeared through the front door.

They reached the corner and crossed the street. It was time. He handed Nathan the key. "Go now, Nathan." Then Kersey turned to face Rose. She bolted across the street. A look of shock, then fear raced across her face.

Kersey felt smug, thinking he'd frightened her into stopping this wild pursuit. Then something exploded against the back of his head. The blow sent stars twirling around his head like a cartoon. He dropped to his knees, glanced back, and recognized the two men from the speeding car the day before. They'd brought two friends with them.

He spotted Nathan standing a few feet away, not sure of what to do. Kersey yelled, "Run, Nathan! Run!" To his relief, the boy ran.

CHAPTER SEVENTEEN

One of the men swung a baseball bat at Kersey's head. He blocked the swing, swatting it aside with his hand. He had to clear his head to plan his attack, but the blow had been hard enough to stun him. He dragged one foot underneath and started to rise as another man swung a tire iron. To block it would mean a broken bone, but he had no room to duck. Instead, he dove at the man's legs, wrapped both arms around them and twisted. The iron grazed his back as the man went down.

Someone kicked him in the ribs. Arms still around the man's legs, he rolled him on top. That gave him a second's reprieve from the attack. He kicked out, connecting with the side of a knee. It buckled and the man staggered away, fighting for balance.

With two men out of the fight, if only for the moment, he shoved the man on top, rolled away, then leaped to his feet. He caught a punch to the face before countering with a quick but powerful jab. The man's head snapped back. His eyes rolled up and he went down to his knees.

Pain shot up his leg as the man with the tire iron connected. Kersey danced away, then planted a foot and stomped on the downed man's chest. He doubled over as air burst from his lungs. The man threw a haymaker. Kersey leaned back to avoid the blow and fired a right cross to the jaw. The man crumbled to the ground like a house of cards.

His mind raced for a fighting sequence to end the brawl, but before he could implement the plan, another explosion erupted behind his eyes and he went down, blacking out before his face connected with the cement.

Nathan hurried to the house holding the key out in front of him so he wouldn't lose it. So many thoughts and fears raced through his mind and he couldn't focus on any of them. However, one notion kept returning. Ker-sey was in trouble. Ker-sey was his friend. He was a superhero. He would save his friend Ker-sey.

His hand shook as he aimed it toward the lock. It took both hands to slide the key home. He twisted the key and turned the knob, but the door did not open. "Oh no." He studied the door, then remembered there were two locks. He slid the key into the deadbolt and turned. Now the door opened.

"Ker-sey in trouble. Must save Ker-sey." He went upstairs as fast as he could, exhausted from his run. He burst through his bedroom door and searched frantically for the Super Me costume. Unable to find it, he raised both hands and shouted, "No!"

He tossed things around, hoping the costume would appear. "Ker-sey in trouble. Must save Ker-sey." He growled with frustration. The costume was nowhere to be seen. "How I save Ker-sey?" Then a thought came to him. He had superpowers. He pointed toward his head. "X-ray vision." He scanned the room again, keeping the finger at his temple like it was the on button for x-ray vision.

He caught a glimpse of red hanging from the laundry hamper. "Yesssh!" He pumped his fist and ripped open the lid, tossing it aside. He pulled the costume out and began getting ready to save his friend.

Dressed and ready as Super Me, Nathan went down the stairs and to the front door. He pulled it open to find his mother coming up the stairs. Nathan ran outside. "Mommy!" He wrapped his arms around her, almost knocking her from the stairs.

"Ah, how nice. Did you miss me?"

"Yuh." Then he released her and ran past her down the stairs. "See you later."

"Wait! Nathan! Where are you going?'

"To save Ker-sey."

"What? Where's Kersey?"

"Bad man and lady hurt him. Must save Ker-sey." He galloped down the street.

"Nathan!" she shouted after him.

"Not Nathan! Super Me!" he yelled back, arms out in front of himself like he was flying.

Nathan raced down the street. He stepped off the curb at the first crosswalk, but then remembered what his mother, Mrs. Wilson, and Ker-sey said about looking both ways and stopped. After checking for cars, he darted across the street.

Behind him he heard his mother calling, but he could not stop. Ker-sey needed him. He ran on. At the end of the next block, the bad lady stood with a man. The man held a large thing on his shoulder that looked like a space gun. But he didn't see Ker-sey.

As he approached, the lady noticed. The man spun around and aimed the space gun at Nathan. He ran on, believing he was immune to the gun's death ray. Nathan stopped a few feet short of the two and placed hands on hips. He looked around. Ker-sey was missing.

"Oh, that's perfect," the bad lady said.

Nathan lifted his arms to the side, palms up. "Where Ker-sey?"

"Those men took him."

"Men—took him? How I gonna save him?"

"What's your name?" She put a microphone in Nathan's face.

"I'm Super Me. You the bad lady."

"Me? I'm a bad lady?"

"Yuh."

"Why am I bad?"

He thought for a moment before saying, "'Cause you do bad things. You help the bad men take my friend."

Before she could continue, Nathan's mother arrived. "What's going on here?" She spotted the microphone. "Get that out of my son's face." She pointed at the camera. "And you have no right to record him. Turn that off now."

"Rose Panera, Channel Ten News. You're Super Me's mother?"

"She bad lady. She took Ker-sey."

Janelle looked at Rose. "Where's Kersey?"

"Four men attacked him, knocked him out, and carted him away."

Janelle's mouth moved wordlessly before she found her voice. "Did you call the police?'

The color drained from Rose's face.

"Oh, that's great. You were more interested in a story than the danger Kersey was in. You're a real humanitarian." She looked into the camera. "Did you get that? Bet that won't make the news. And if I see one second of my son on TV, I'm suing you personally." She took Nathan by the arm and led him away. She took out her phone and dialed 911. "A man was assaulted and kidnapped." She gave her location and Kersey's name and description, then added, "A reporter, Rose Pantera from Channel Ten, filmed the entire thing but didn't think it was important enough to call it in." Her voice was loud enough to be heard.

They waited for the police on the porch. Rose and her cameraman were gone. The two officers exited the car and approached. The taller man said, "We're making this a habit, aren't we?"

"Excuse me?" Janelle said.

"We were here yesterday. A neighbor reported a possible intruder."

"So who's the kidnap victim?" the shorter cop asked.

"The man you came to investigate. His name is Kersey. I'm not sure what his last name is."

"You had a stranger watching your child?" The tall cop asked.

"He's not a stranger. I, we, ah…" But anything she said would only make it look worse. "Look, that doesn't matter. A reporter, Rose Pantera, filmed the entire assault and took off."

"She didn't call it in?" the taller cop asked.

"Guess she felt the story was more important than a man's life."

The two cops looked at each and shook their heads in disbelief.

Nathan tugged on the shorter cop's shirt. "We save Ker-sey."

"Ah yeah, sure."

"No," he said more emphatically. "We save Ker-sey now."

The cop pulled his arm away. "We will, but we need more information first."

"What more can I tell you? He's a big man. It would take a lot to take him down."

"Yuh," Nathan said. "He strong." He flexed. "Like me." He counted out three fingers, thought for a moment, and lifted one more. "This many bad guys."

"Four?" the taller cop asked.

"Yuh." He swung his arms. "Use bat. Hit Ker-sey on head."

If the cops hadn't taken Nathan seriously before, they did now. The details made the story more credible.

CHAPTER EIGHTEEN

"Joe, you better call it in," the taller cop said. "I'll get what else I can."

Joe turned away and spoke into his shoulder mic. The remaining officer asked Janelle, "Can you tell me anything else about the assailants? Did Kersey have a problem with anyone?"

"I wasn't there when it happened. Nathan knows more than I do. I was in the hospital. I wasn't here when Kersey arrived. He doesn't live here. I can't imagine he had a problem with anyone here, unless one followed him."

"What does Kersey do?"

"Do?"

"Yeah. His job."

"Well, that's hard to say."

"Ker-sey a superhero. Like me," Nathan said.

"Is that right?" the cop said.

"I guess you'd call him a consultant," Janelle added quickly.

"Like with technology?"

"Ah, yeah. People call him up when they have, ah, computer problems, and he fixes them."

A look of suspicion furrowed the cop's brows. "Are you saying he's a troubleshooter?"

Janelle was relieved. "Yes. Exactly."

"But not for computers. Is he someone you'd hire to handle personal problems?"

Janelle felt her stomach drop. She didn't know what to say.

"'Cause if you did, that changes things a lot."

"How does it change a man being beaten and taken?"

"Because if he's a professional, he may have a lot of enemies. If he's here on a job, it might have backfired on him. We might go looking for a kidnap victim and find ourselves in the middle of a drug war or something."

"He only came into town because I called him to watch Nathan. That's the only job he was here to do."

"Okay. Is there anything else you can tell us to help find Kersey?"

"I don't know. Like what?"

"Like type of vehicle the attackers were driving." Something about the question started Nathan's wheels in motion. He worried at the answer for a moment.

"Like I said, I wasn't there."

"Okay. If you think of anything else, please contact us."

"A van!" Nathan blurted. "They have van."

"Who did?" asked the cop.

"Bad guys."

The cop nodded. "Do you remember the color?"

"Yuh."

The cop waited.

"Tell him the color, Nathan."

"White."

"A white van? You're sure?"

"Yuh." He spread his arms wide. "Big one."

Joe returned. "Guess the reporter didn't waste any time airing the story. They interrupted their normal shows. It's like the boy—"

"Nathan," Janelle said.

"Yes, sorry. Like Nathan said, there was four of them. One had a bat; another a tire iron. He took a few good shots before going down. Department's sending some of the brass to the station to meet with the manager."

"I think we've got all we need for now," said the taller cop. "Let's canvass a bit and see if anyone else saw something." To Janelle, he said, "We'll be in touch."

The officers jogged down the steps and drove away. Janelle took Nathan's hand to lead him inside, but he pulled away.

"No, Mommy. We save Ker-sey. He in trouble." He spread his arms wide again. "Big trouble."

"We've done all we can for now. We have to let the police do their jobs. We can't get in the way. There's nothing we can do until the police find him."

Nathan didn't like the answer and allowed his mother to coax him into the house, but that didn't stop him from planning. He had to help his friend. Superheroes helped each other and he had to help Ker-sey. He just couldn't figure out how.

An idea came to him. He had super powers. He could fly and find Ker-sey from the sky. That was the answer. He had to get someplace high so he could fly above the houses. But where was the highest place he knew? His bedroom.

He could jump out the window.

"Hang on, Ker-sey. Super Me coming to save you."

With that, he ran up the stairs and into his room.

CHAPTER NINETEEN

Kersey woke in painful increments. His head and face hurt. An attempt to open his eyes failed and brought additional pain. He wanted to shake his head to clear his mind but knew to do so would only create more excruciating pain.

He was unable to move his hands or feet. Since he was sitting, he figured he was bound to a chair. With care, he opened his eyes. Only one took in any light, but any image was too blurred to identify. He blinked several times before the scene came into focus.

The room was small; perhaps ten by twelve. It had a ragged carpet, dingy walls, and a foul odor. It looked like a bedroom, but there was no bed. Light filtered in through a window covered with cardboard.

A sudden rush of anxiety struck and he turned his head to take in the room. Nathan was not there, meaning he either got away or was being held in another room. He flexed to test his bonds. They were tight but given enough time, he'd get free. He started flexing hard and relaxing to stretch the cords out. It didn't take long to gain some wiggle room.

The sound of voices made him pause. Somewhere in an outer room, an argument was in full swing. Though he couldn't make out the words, the tone told him there was dissention in the ranks. That was good. He might be able to use that to his advantage.

Kersey went back to work on the cords. He discovered they had bound his hands with duct tape first. Then the rope was added. The rope was the soft kind, like clothesline. That made a tighter knot but let his hands spin, especially with the rope over the tape. They were not pros; that much was certain.

Someone screamed and there was a crash. The shouting intensified. The words were clearer.

"It's all over the news! We can't go anywhere!"

The cameraman must have recorded the assault and Rose Pantera put it on air. That was good and bad. Good, because the police would have a place to start the hunt. Bad, because keeping him alive might not be the best thing to do. He increased his efforts.

"What are we going to do?" another voice shouted.

"First thing is to stay calm," a third voice said.

"Stay calm?" the screamer said. "Are you nuts? We have to get out of here now!"

"What about him?"

Kersey stopped working to hear better. This was important. He needed to know their intentions toward him. The voices got quiet. Whoever called for calm had won out. Now Kersey no longer heard the conversation. He went back to work with increased effort.

He managed to angle his hands so he had an end of the rope between his fingers. He traced it down to the knot and began worrying it loose. He had the top knot separated and a minute later a door slammed. Kersey froze. Then the door to the room opened and two men entered. They walked with a purpose, like they'd already decided his fate. He was out of time.

He recognized the two men from the confrontation on the street. Their eyes were hard and bore straight through him. That didn't bode well. If he was going down, he wasn't about to make it easy for them. As they closed the distance, the front man reached behind him. A gun would be in his hand when it came back out. Kersey had seconds to act.

He rocked back on the chair's rear legs, then leaned forward. As the chair dropped he gained momentum, landing his feet, and stood hunched over. The men paused. Then, he shuffle ran at the front man, surprising him. Though his hand reappeared holding something, Kersey plowed forward. He lowered his head and rammed the man, knocking him backward off his feet. However, the collision caused his bound legs to become entangled with the falling man's. He tripped. Unable to protect himself from the fall, he face planted on the filthy carpet. The contact sent a wave of fresh pain through him. He rolled on his side, seeing a spray of his blood added to the other stains.

He tried to kick to regain his feet but being on his side left him with few options. He was unable to get back to his feet or get into a position where he might headbutt, kick, or bite. The second man pounded a fist into the side of his head. He was an easy target now.

The man on the floor scooted away, then pushed to his feet. He stepped forward and landed a kick to Kersey's chest. The blow flipped him on to his back. He caught sight of an object lowering toward him. This was the end. He was going to take a shot point-blank to the head.

But he wasn't defenseless. In desperation, he focused. Even though he had no target to hit, he hoped whatever happened would be enough of a distraction to give him some options. He released a power blast against the floor. The force of air served as propulsion and lifted him into the air.

One of the men said, "Whoa!"

The other, "What the—"

But what goes up must come down, especially after slamming into the ceiling. Kersey had no way to prevent the crash landing. He hit and bounced. The front legs of the chair hit first and snapped. Though his legs were now free, he had no chance to avoid the contact. He deflected the chair from another frontal impact on his face, flipping onto his back. His head whipped back and cracked against the floor. The lights went dim. He fought to clear his mind and his vision. In the faint light that filtered through his eyes, he saw a hand descend toward him. He heard a zap. His body convulsed and darkness came.

Nathan stood perched on the window sill of his second-floor bedroom. He looked down and swallowed hard. It was a long way down. He was afraid. He stepped back into the room. "Too high," he said. Then, he got angry with himself. "No. Not too high. You superhero. Super Me!" he yelled, lifting his arms up. "Ker-sey need help. You fly."

He climbed back to the sill and squatted awkwardly. "Don't look down. Look up. Yuh. Up." He stared, mesmerized by the thought of soaring above the houses.

"Nathan!" his mother called from downstairs. Startled, he turned to answer her. His foot slipped. For a moment he hovered in space, one foot still in contact with the sill. Then he plummeted, falling so fast he had no time to scream.

CHAPTER TWENTY

His body bounced, smacking against something solid a short distance over him. He landed with a jolt. The impacts roused him to consciousness with a groan. It took a moment and another body-bouncing bump to realize he was in the trunk of a car. His hands and feet bound, Kersey quickly went to work on gaining his freedom. The time he needed was cut short as seconds later, the car slowed, then stopped.

Kersey attempted to position his large body with his hands toward the trunk latch. He wanted to unleash his power at whoever opened the trunk. However, the space was too small to allow much movement and his well-muscled body proved too bulky to maneuver.

Doors opened and closed. The car rocked with the exodus. A conversation ensued. Accented voices responded. Where had they brought him? Keys scratched at the lock. The lid lifted. Light poured in. With the impediment removed, Kersey rolled. He drew in his power, expanding his lungs. He couldn't see where he aimed, but envisioned hands reaching for him and gave a reasonable idea where his enemies might be. Before he could release the blast, the hard, cold barrel was placed against his cheek.

"Come out of there very slowly," an accented voice said.

He released the hold on his power, hoping for a better opportunity, and scooted forward. Kersey swung his legs over the edge of the trunk. The man standing there wore a tight pullover shirt that accentuated bulky muscles. He held an H&K .45 pointed at Kersey's face. Another man held a gun and stood to the side.

Though his stature was smaller, the look in his dark eyes spoke volumes. He was a stone-cold killer.

Fifteen feet away was a heavyset man in an expensive suit standing near a Cadillac limo. His hair lifted with the breeze. He wore a sinister smug on his fleshy face and stood with the air of a man with everything under his control. To his side were the kidnappers. Their nervous glances to each other said they felt as out of place as they looked with the other three men.

What had he fallen into this time?

The muscled man motioned for Kersey to slide out of the trunk. As soon as his feet touched ground, he drew in energy; energy that would be transferred to a power he tried not to use, but he knew the time had come. Since discovering his ability five years earlier, he had used it only four times, and only then when absolutely necessary.

The well-dressed man that Kersey figured for the boss took a step forward. "Ah, Mr. Kersey," he said. Kersey now recognized the accent as Russian. He felt the beginning of an icy chill creep through his veins. "I'm so glad it is you. I've been looking for you for a while. Ever since you killed my brother."

Oh, man! This was Larionov's brother. He *had* killed the man. The Russian gangster had kidnapped Nathan. Kersey had no regrets putting the evil man down, but he had a feeling this brother was even worse.

The two armed men moved to either side of Kersey, both keeping their distance.

The boss said, "I don't know how you managed to wipe out an entire wing of my organization, but I'm going to find out. Then, you will die. It will be fun—at least for me."

One of the original captors said, "See, ah, sir, it's like I said. It's the man you wanted."

"Yes. I am in your debt." He tapped on the limo's window and it rolled down. A pale face poked out. "Yes sir?"

"Pay them."

"As you wish, sir."

The door opened and a tall, rail-thin man exited. He reached into an inside jacket pocket and the kidnappers gasped and took a step back. The tall man and his boss exchanged glances and smiles. He held a large manila envelope. He handed it to the kidnapper who spoke. He accepted it with a shaky hand.

The boss said, "I have reports that a large black woman aided this man. Find her, and the pay will double."

"Ah, yes sir. Sure."

The kidnappers whirled around and almost ran to the car. The doors slammed and the car raced away, leaving Kersey to face the mobsters.

"Now, Mr. Kersey, if you would oblige me by getting into my trunk. It should be roomier than your previous accommodations." He gave a bark of laughter, then motioned to his men.

Kersey needed the men to get close together to use his power to its fullest advantage. If he only took one of them out, the remaining man would shoot. But they were either too well trained or knew about his ability. Had one of the men he took down before survived his attack? That would be the only way they could know.

The men worked him to the trunk. The lid popped open. Boss man was right. This was a three body trunk. He had plenty of room to maneuver this time. He climbed in the best he could with his hands bound. As he settled in, the smaller man moved fast and jabbed a taser into his back. His body convulsed, but he stayed aware until the second jolt. He wasn't sure, since he was slipping into unconsciousness, but he thought the man zapped him a third time. As the trunk closed and his vision faded, his last conscious sight was the most sinister smile he'd ever seen.

CHAPTER TWENTY-ONE

Nathan hovered four feet off the ground. He opened his eyes and saw he hadn't pancaked on the driveway, then let out a whoop of joy. "Yuh!" He was flying. He extended his arms like he had with Kersey, but something was wrong. He wasn't moving. Try as he might, he was stuck in one place. Then he fell. He smacked into the cement. His hands drew back underneath him in time to prevent his face from slamming into the hard surface, but his knees and elbows hit hard and his chin took a scrape.

It hurt. It hurt bad enough to cry, but he fought back the tears. He was Super Me and superheroes didn't cry. Still, fat tears trailed down his cheeks as he rolled to his bottom, drew up his knees, and caressed them to relieve the pain.

Overhead, the voice of his mother drifted through the open window. "Nathan, answer me!" She would come upstairs when he didn't answer. If she looked out the window and saw him there, she'd be mad. He didn't want her to yell. She'd make him stay in the house, and he had to find Ker-sey.

He rolled to his hands and knees, but the contact with the driveway caused more pain. He gasped and sobbed but adjusted his position and pushed to his feet. As he stood, he looked at his hands. Long scrapes marked each palm. Blood seeped from a deeper groove in his left hand. He winced at the sight and gasped again as he tried to wipe his hands clean on his black sweat pants.

Glancing down, he noticed both knees of the pants now had tears in them. Mommy was going to be really, really mad. He hurried down the driveway, wincing audibly. His knees hurt too. Being a superhero was hard work.

He reached the place where the driveway sloped toward the street. Before he could descend, an arm shot out from the bushes in Mrs. Bitner's front yard, gripped his arm, and jerked him off his feet. A shout of surprise escaped his mouth before a hand clamped down over his mouth.

Lips pressed against his ear and whispered. "Shh! I won't hurt you. I'm a friend of Kersey's. I'm here to find him." She turned him so he could see her. He recognized her and his eyes went wide.

"You remember me, don't you?"

His head bobbed vigorously.

"My name's Aleeyah. I need your help to find Kersey. Will you help me?"

Again, he nodded with zeal.

"I'm going to take my hand away from your mouth, but I need you to remain quiet. Okay?"

"Yuh!" he said into her hand.

She smiled and removed her hand. "Can you lead me to where Kersey was taken?"

"Yuh."

"Good. Let's go."

"Nathan!" a loud voice shouted from the upstairs window full of worry and concern. With hands over her face, Janelle looked down, then put a hand to her chest.

Nathan drew in a breath to answer his mommy, but the hand closed off the words. He struggled for a moment until the lips were back at his ear. "If your mother sees you, she won't let you help me."

Nathan thought about that, then calmed down, relaxing his body in her grasp.

"Good boy."

His mother called again. "Where are you, young man? This is no time to be playing hide and seek. Come here now!"

He looked up. His mother was no longer standing in the window. Aleeyah said, "Now." She hoisted him to his feet and began jogging. She was too fast for Nathan and he stumbled and almost fell. Her strong arms hauled him to his feet. "You have to keep up. This will only take a minute. Then I'll have you back home."

They jogged to a dark SUV like Ker-sey drove. She opened the passenger door and shoved him in. Seconds later they were driving away from the house. Nathan looked back over the seat. "Mommy very angry."

"I'm sorry, Nathan, but I really need your help. I promise I'll bring you right back. Can you show me where the bad men took Kersey?"

"Yuh."

"What direction?"

Nathan turned in his seat again. "There."

"The other direction?"

"Yuh."

Aleeyah made a series of turns and came back to Nathan's street one block in the opposite direction. "Now where?"

"There." He pointed.

Nathan guided her to the spot.

"Okay. I need to send a message to your mother so she won't worry. Do you know your phone number?"

"Yuh." He placed a hand on his forehead as if that helped him think, then recited the number.

Aleeyah spoke as she texted a message. *Nathan is safe and with me. I'm a friend of Kersey's He is helping me find him. I will have him back shortly. I will keep him safe.* She didn't add her name.

"Will that help?"

Nathan grimaced and shrugged.

"Okay, let's do this."

CHAPTER TWENTY-TWO

_____

Aleeyah exited and helped Nathan out. "This is the spot?"

"Yuh."

"Tell me what happened."

"Bad men come. They hit Ker-sey with a bat." He made the motion of swinging a bat. "Ker-sey fall down. He say, 'Nathan.' That's me. 'Run.'"

"And you did?"

Nathan paused, then said, "No. I stay to help, but Ker-sey yell again. Other bad man hit him with—" he tried to explain but evidently didn't know what the bad guy used. He shrugged then made the swinging motion again.

"Did you see anything else?"

"No. I run. Get my superhero costume, then run back to help Ker-sey."

"Think, Nathan. Did you see or hear anything else?"

Nathan placed a hand to his forehead again but shook his head.

"What about a vehicle?"

"Vehicle?" He looked perplexed, then grew animated. "A van. There was a vehicle van."

"What color?"

"White."

"White. Good. Anything else."

"Yuh, big letters." He swung his arms wide to indicate. "On the side."

Big letters. Aleeyah wondered if Nathan knew his letters. She pulled out her cell phone and called up the video she'd seen of the news report aired on TV. Though she hadn't gotten it all, she did have enough to see the takedown. She made the picture wider. At the fringe of the image was a partial view of a van. The only letters she could see were a W and an L. It came to her fast. WLQR were the call letters for the TV station. This didn't help. She sighed. She had to see the original footage of the abduction. Kersey was way too big to drag down a street. The abductors had to have a vehicle nearby.

She looked down at Nathan's eager face. He smiled at her. It was enough to melt even her heart. His eyes scrunched up and his face lit like a lightbulb.

"Did I do good?"

She smiled back. "Yes, Nathan, you did good."

She scanned the area for any security cameras and found one across the street over a pawn shop. If the police knew they already had film of the attack, they might not have checked any other sources. It was a place to start and easier to get to than the TV station, but first she had to return Nathan before his mother called the cops.

"Okay, superhero. Time to go home."

Nathan shook his head. "Not home. We find Ker-sey."

"We can't just yet. I have to check a few things first. Then I'll come back for you. Right now, I have to get you home. You don't want your mommy to worry, do you?"

Nathan thought about it before shaking his head. "No."

As they drove back, Aleeyah wondered how to explain to Nathan that he could not fly. She had taken a job that by a stroke of fortune was less than an hour away. As soon as she saw the TV report, she drove straight here, arriving just as the boy perched on the window sill. If she wouldn't have been there, he'd be dead. She reached out with her mind, created a large air-hand, and caught him. She was going to lift him back to the window and deposit him inside but realized he would think he flew on his own and try it again, so she dropped him from a height just high enough to cause pain, yet not enough to do any real damage.

She pulled to the side of the street a block from his house. "Nathan, I have to tell you something very important." He continued to stare out the window. "Are you listening?'

"Yuh."

"Never ever jump out a window again. Do you hear me? You can't fly."

"Yuh-huh."

"No!" she said louder than intended. His head snapped back; his eyes wide. "You can't fly. I caught you. If I wasn't there, you would have been hurt very badly. You remember falling? And hurting your knees and elbows?"

He looked at his torn sweatpants. "Yuh. Hurt."

"That's right. Hurt. If you do something like that again, you will be hurt very badly. You will have to go to the hospital. Your mother will be very sad and cry for you. You don't want to make her cry, do you?"

He shook his head, tears welling.

"It will also make Kersey angry with you. He doesn't want you to get hurt. He won't want to come see you again."

A tear rolled down his plump cheek.

"You have to promise me and Kersey that you will never jump from a window again. Will you promise?"

He wiped his face and lowered his head to his chest. His lower lip stuck out and quivered. "But I superhero. Superheroes fly."

"No, not all of them. Kersey is a superhero, but he doesn't fly. You want to be like him, don't you?"

He nodded.

"Then you have to promise me not to try to fly again..." An idea struck. "...unless Kersey is there with you. Okay?"

His head came up as he understood. "I fly with Kersey?"

"Yes, but only then. Do you promise?"

"Yuh." He wiped his eyes.

"Okay. Good. Pinky-swear on your promise." She held up a hand with her pinky extended. He looked at it, confused. "Here. Make a fist." She closed his hand. "Now lift your little finger." She put it in place. "Now we shake." She wrapped her much bigger finger around his and gave it a quick pump. "Now the promise is binding."

"Like superhero secret handshake?"

Aleeyah couldn't contain the laugh. "Yes, exactly like that. Now, let's get you home."

CHAPTER TWENTY-THREE

Aleeyah watched him enter his house. Sha hadn't realized she was smiling until she glanced in the mirror. The boy was likeable—big praise from her, but there was also something more to him, something hidden deep inside, almost as if he possessed...no. She shook her head clear and focused on finding Kersey. Aleeyah returned to the pawn shop. It took all of five minutes to entice the owner to share the video with her. Well, five minutes, a little flirting, and the point of her knife under his chin. After that, he was very obliging.

She viewed the grainy footage three times before finding what she wanted—what the TV report hadn't shown—the make, model, and partial plate of the getaway vehicle. Aleeyah planted a kiss on the owner's cheek, set a twenty dollar bill on the counter, and exited.

She had a starting place. A phone call to a source and a fifty dollar donation got the full plate number and the name and address of the owner. Fifteen minutes and three drive-bys later, Aleeyah was parked down the street from the rundown two-story house in a neighborhood where everyone kept their eyes moving and their heads swiveling.

Though she hadn't seen the car, someone was home. Heavy-metal music blared from an upstairs window. From the condition of the structure she wondered how long before the vibrations would shake the house to the ground. She waited a while, but several passersby had already marked her as an alien in their world. She moved the car three blocks down. In the mirror over the visor, she checked her spiked pink hair and added more shocking pink lipstick, then hiked back.

Without hesitation, she turned up the front walk to the steps like she belonged there. She pretended to have a key and in seconds was inside. The music was deafening. She scanned the shabby interior. Worn second-hand furniture filled the front room to the left. Dirty clothes and empty food containers covered everything.

Another room was attached to the front room, but whatever its original purpose was lost to the collection of broken down electronic equipment and automotive parts strewn about the floor and counters.

To the right was a staircase leading up. Straight ahead, a short hallway led to the kitchen. She went that way. If the front room was messy, this was a disaster. Dirty plates were piled in the sink and on every flat surface. Pizza cartons, some still containing slices, were strewn around the room, spilling over to the faded tile floor.

No one was in any of the rooms.

Aleeyah went upstairs, unconcerned about the loud squeaks. No one would hear over the music. She stood at the top of the stairs and studied the hall before her. Four doors, two on each side. One had to be the bathroom. One door on the far right was open. The source of the auditory assault was the near left. A dim light shone beneath the door.

She approached, turned the knob, and peered through the crack. A shirtless long haired man lay on the bed, beating his bare chest with drumsticks to the beat of the raging noise. His eyes were closed.

Aleeyah recognized him from the video. He swung the bat. Instant rage flared within her core, but she held it in check. She needed information before she did any damage. She entered and closed the door behind her.

Lifting a long muscular leg, she leaped and landed on the bed, straddling the drummer boy. The impact lifted him. She caught his face between her hands, squeezed, and flashed a brilliant smile.

The man struggled, but she quickly ended his efforts with a tighter squeeze on his face. "Relax. Relax. You should be happy, not worried. I doubt you've ever had anyone this hot in your bed before."

"Did Bobby and Joey send you?"

"Oh no, honey. Nobody sends me. I just arrive. Then the party begins."

At the mention of party, he relaxed. "Well, all right. Let's party."

She pushed his head down into the filthy lump he called a pillow. "Oh, first things first, baby. And that first thing is you're gonna tell me what you did with my friend."

A look of confusion crossed his narrow face. "Friend? What friend?"

"Oh, you know what friend. The one you clubbed with a baseball bat."

His eyes widened. Fear sucked the air from his lungs. "I-I don't know what you're talking about."

"You don't?" Her voice remained calm and sweet. "Let me refresh your memory. You and three of your cowardly friends jumped him from behind. You hit him with a bat and a tire iron. Now, I'm here to rescue him—something I will never let him forget, but first you have to tell me where he is."

"Lady, I—"

"The next words out of your mouth had better be where I can find him, or..." With a quick flick of her hand, a six-inch blade snapped open. "I'm going to begin removing body parts. I'll start with parts you don't have any use for, like these." She reached back and put the point between his legs.

He squealed and began blathering in a long run-on sentence.

"Whoa, baby. Slow your roll. Now tell me what you did with him."

"We sold him to this guy."

Alarms went off in her head. "Sold him? To what guy?" All sweetness fled her tone.

"I-I don't know. Some guy said he saw the story on TV and tracked us down. He was willing to pay big bucks, providing your friend wasn't hurt."

"Tell me about him."

"Older guy. Lots of money and power. Spoke with an accent."

"What type of accent?"

"I don't know."

The tip of the blade pierced skin. The man arched back and howled. "No! No! Please!"

"What kind of accent?"

"I think it was Russian."

That brought Aleeyah up short like a slap to the face. Russian? Could there be a connection to their last mission here a month back? Had to be. "What else?"

"He said something about it being payback for messing with his brother and his organization."

Confirmation. Kersey was taken by a Russian mobster. "How long ago was the exchange?"

"Earlier today. About three hours ago."

"Why did you take him in the first place?"

"We got into a spat with him yesterday. We went back to even the score."

"Using four guys? That was very brave. So this Russian wasn't why you took him?"

"No. We got caught on video and didn't know what to do. When this guy contacted us, it seemed the easiest solution."

Not good. Not good at all. She questioned him further, digging the point of the blade in deeper when she got no more information. He was crying and swore he'd tell her if he knew anything more.

She swung her leg off the man and he instantly curled into the fetal position with his hands cupped between his legs. "You'd better pray he's still alive, or I'll come back and carve you to pieces."

She stomped out of the room but stopped and went back. She flipped the bed with her mind, then dropped it on top of him. Three times. She jogged down the stairs, reaching the bottom as the front door burst open and three obviously stoned men stumbled in carrying two large pizzas. They saw her and broke into a laughing spell. One yelled up the stairs, "Man, Daryl! You couldn't wait for us to get back to call the hookers?"

Though it might have been smarter to question them, when she left, they were in no condition to speak. She took one of the pizzas with her.

CHAPTER TWENTY-FOUR

Evidently, the Russian mobster thought he would be out for the duration of the trip, because he hadn't bothered cutting out the yellow trunk release cord hanging above Kersey's head. That discovery gave him an idea.

His power only worked when summoned through his hands. In truth, he wasn't positive, but that's how he'd always used his strange ability since he discovered it almost two years ago. Early attempts to use only his mind had failed, and he hadn't bothered exploring other options. Now was not the time for experimenting. Once he broke out, if he couldn't free his hands, he'd have to keep his back to the enemy. That meant firing blindly if he was running. He hoped the distraction of the sudden mysterious assault would create enough gap for him to escape. Perhaps a car would appear and whisk him to safety.

An escape was a gamble but staying in the trunk would only lead to torture and death, so it was worth the risk. He ran the plan through his mind. He had to get the trunk open and roll out as fast as possible to gain a lead. That meant as soon as the trunk lid lifted, he had to be ready to go. The landing would hurt. There was no way around that, but he had to absorb the pain throughout his body by rolling. If his head hit or broke a leg or ankle, the effort would be for nothing.

He gathered his power, then his nerve. He gripped and pulled the plastic release cord with his teeth. A thump sounded, air rushed in, and the lid lifted. Kersey leaned over the lip and saw the road rushing beneath him. He swallowed hard and raised a leg into open air. Before he completed the drop, the car slowed. He'd been spotted.

Faster than intended, he went airborne. As he fell, he used a short burst of power to slow the fall, but though it had the desired effect, it flipped him through the air. He landed on his left shoulder with a painful jolt. He rolled, though not of his own volition. Keeping his head from snapping back on the concrete road was not easy, but he managed to avoid serious injury by keeping his neck muscles taut and not allowing his head to whip. He did have abrasions to his face and head. Even his well-honed body could not prevent all contact.

Pain shot up and down his body with each successive roll. Knowing his time was limited, he widened his legs to end the roll, taking more damage to his knees. As soon as he stopped, he got to his feet, which was a task made more difficult with his hands still bound. Ignoring the pain, he took off at a run.

His first steps coincided with the doors opening. Shouts followed him. He wondered how much longer before the bullets would come. The first few shots would be warnings. Then they'd aim to wound—most likely to take out a leg. He ran as fast as he could, waiting to hear the explosions. To his surprise, many more seconds passed before he heard anything, but when he did, it surprised him.

The sound of the car engine getting louder gave him a start. Of course, they'd chase him in the car instead of on foot or shooting. With quick sideways glances, Kersey took in his surroundings. To the right was water—lots of water. It was either a wide river or a huge lake. The water would make escape easier, but without being able to use his hands, he'd drown.

To the left were long buildings. Warehouses. He was at some dock. He scanned the horizon of the water but could not see to the other side. The Atlantic Ocean? Made sense. In the distance, a large freighter made its way toward the docks.

He dodged left and saw a fence surrounding the closest building. He had no way to scale it. The car closed in. He slowed, lifted, and aimed his joined hands behind him, then released a forced air blast. Screeching tires rewarded his efforts, however, not being in a stable position left the backlash uncontrolled. It pitched him head first into the chain link fence. He dropped to his knees, momentarily stunned.

He shook off the effects and climbed to his feet. Behind him he heard the doors open again. "Boris, you trying to kill us? What was that?"

"I don't know. It was like we hit an invisible wall or something."

"Don't just stand there, you fools. Go get him."

That was Kersey's cue to hurry. He ran along the fence line with no clear plan. If he could get his hands free, the fight would be over, but they made sure he was tied tight. His body ached from multiple areas, but he pressed on. The smell of the crisp sea air helped to revitalize him. Footsteps followed. Harder soled shoes echoed off the building and gave him an idea of where they were. Soon they faded. They might be tough, but they weren't in the same physical condition as Kersey.

He reached the end of the fence and turned left. Ahead was open road that went on for perhaps a half mile before it appeared to end. He wondered if water was beyond. Only one way to find out. He notched up his speed to another level. The more distance he put between himself and his pursuers, the better the chance of escaping or at least finding something to cut the rope around his wrists with.

The engine raced, telling him he hadn't caused any permanent damage to the car. He'd have to do better this time. He began drawing in energy and converting it to power. The first shot ricocheted off the roadway three feet to his right. The sound startled him, causing him to release the power prematurely.

He edged left to prevent the shooter from zeroing in on his body. The energy flowed in again. He had never tested the limits of his ability but knew without rest that three was the maximum blasts he could release in a row. He'd used two. This one had to count.

Two more shots chipped up chunks of cement close to his feet. He moved right. The car drew closer. A quick glance over his shoulder gave him a direction to aim. He slowed, wanting to be sure of a score, and lifted his hands, but before he could release the blast, a bullet ripped into his thigh and another creased his head.

Kersey went down fast and hard. His chin bounced. His body slid and the lights went out.

CHAPTER TWENTY-FIVE

Nathan was at the dinner table when the vision came to him. "Owiee!" he screamed, putting a hand to his head and his chin. "Owiee! Owiee! Owiee!" he cried, gripping his leg.

His mother ran into the dining room, an oven mitt on with a hot pot of chicken noodle soup.

"Nathan, what is it? What's wrong?"

He turned his round face up. Tears filled his eyes and rolled down his red cheeks. "Mommy, Ker-sey."

"Kersey? What about Kersey?"

"He hurt. Hurt real bad."

"What do you mean, honey?"

"Ker-sey hurt. Leg burns. Head burns. Face. Right here," he pointed to his chin, "hurt too."

"How do you know this, Nathan?"

"I see it. And I feel it."

"But you're okay, right?"

He stared right through her like she wasn't there. "No," he shook his head slowly.

"Nathan?"

No response. She reached out with her free hand and felt his head for fever. Though sweaty, she felt no heat. In fact, if anything, he felt cool. Nathan rapidly blinked and shook his head. "He's gone, Mommy."

"Who's gone?"

"Ker-sey. He's gone."

"Where did he go?"

He lifted his arms to the side and shrugged. "Don't know. Too dark."

"It was just a dream, Nathan. I'm sure Kersey is okay."

"No, Mommy. Bad men get him. They hurt him more."

"How do you know this?"

"I see." He pointed to his head. "Right in here."

"It was just your imagination, honey. You couldn't have really seen Kersey."

"Yuh-huh. It real. Ker-sey in bad trouble." He pushed the chair back and got up.

"Wait! Where you going?"

"Call Lee-ah. She save Ker-sey before it's too late."

"Nathan, sit down and have your dinner. We can talk about this while we eat."

He stomped his foot. "No, Mommy. Have to call Lee-ah now. Right now." He crossed his arms and glared at her.

Janelle was used to Nathan's little outbursts, though he hadn't had one in a while, but something about this one was different. It bordered on complete meltdown. Though he hadn't had many, she knew it might take the better part of the night to calm him.

The hard look in his eyes and the determined set of his jaw were new. He also was just standing there, tapping his foot like his patience was wearing thin. His usual meltdowns were all wild fury. He stomped, screamed, flailed, threw things, and tossed himself around like a beachball. She needed to be firm yet keep him calm.

"Nathan!" she hardened her voice. "Sit down and we will discuss this. I will not listen until you sit down."

He shook his head slowly. "No, Mommy." He took a deep breath, then a quiet but firm voice said, "Mom."

Mom! Though she'd tried many times to get him to switch from Mommy, he never called her Mom. He held out his hand. "Give me phone now."

Something about his demeanor caught her attention. He was calm yet determined. The serious expression showed true concern for Kersey. She didn't doubt he was in trouble wherever he was, but Nathan couldn't possibly have seen the circumstances.

She slid the mitt from her hand, placed it on the table, and set the pot on top. She squatted in front of Nathan and took his hands. "Nathan, what you saw was your imagination creating an image of Kersey. You probably remember a TV show like that and put Kersey's face on the hero."

"No, Mom. It real." He stomped his foot again and pulled his hands from her grasp, then stuck out his hand. "Phone, Mommy. Please."

She studied her son for a long moment, wondering the best way to proceed. Nathan stepped forward and placed a hand on each side of her face. He looked her in the eyes and said, "You wrong, Mommy. This real. Not my 'magination. I see Ker-sey. He needs my help. Trust me."

It was the first time he'd ever said that to her. He looked so serious so—grown up. She found that she did trust him. She might not believe what he saw but loved the fact he was willing to stand up for it.

"I don't have her number."

"Yes, Mom. You do."

He'd never said yes properly. He sounded so mature. What was going on here?

"She text you. 'Member?"

"Oh, that's right." He had called her bluff. "Okay, let's call her."

She retrieved the phone from her purse, found the text, and sent a message. *Nathan would like to speak with you.* She thought about adding an explanation but decided to let Nathan do that.

"There. I sent her a message. Now, why don't we eat while we wait for her to call back?"

He nodded. "Yuh."

CHAPTER TWENTY-SIX

Aleeyah didn't have time to waste to call Nathan. He probably just wanted an update on Kersey anyway. She had to move forward, but in truth had no path to follow. All she knew for sure was members of the Russian mob had him. Where they were holding him was anyone's guess. She couldn't lose precious time searching blindly or making calls to Nathan.

She called a contact and gave him Larionov's name and then asked him to find any holdings he or the Russian mob might have within a hundred miles of her location. They agreed on a fee and Aleeyah said, "Bonus for getting info back to me within the hour."

She sat in the SUV and tapped the phone against her lip as she thought of other avenues of pursuit. Instead, her mind drifted to Nathan. He was a sweet boy and was concerned about Kersey, but did she want to get any more involved? The message had obviously come from the mother. Perhaps she wanted Aleeyah to assure the boy that Kersey was all right.

She reread the message and started a text reply, but then had a different thought. She called the number. She wanted to remind Nathan not to fly anymore. She didn't want his injury or death to weigh on her conscience.

The phone was answered on the third ring. "Hello?" the mother said.

"You texted me."

"Yes, I did. Look, I know you have more important things to do, but Nathan has convinced himself that he saw Kersey, and that he is not only in trouble but hurt, as well. I'd appreciate it if you could back me up on this and just tell him...I don't know...that he was mistaken or something."

Silence.

Then Aleeyah said, "Put him on."

"Thank you."

"Lee-ah, Ker-sey hurt real bad."

"He is?"

"Yuh. Pain in head and chin. Burning on leg."

"How do you know this, Nathan?" she asked, her attention caught on a prior thought.

"I see him. Bad men hurt him. He fall down. Then it dark."

Could it be possible the boy actually saw Kersey? She had sensed something in the boy but had shrugged it off as a false read. "You really saw him?"

"Yuh. We save him. You Super Me too."

The statement froze her for a moment. Did he actually know she had abilities, or was he just saying that because she helped him before? "What do you mean?"

"You know, Lee-ah. We both superheroes."

"Ah, right. I forgot."

"Come get me. We save Ker-sey together."

In the background, she heard his mother say, "Oh no, Nathan. You're not leaving this house again alone."

"Mom!" he said, the exasperation in his tone coming through the phone.

"No, and that's final."

Nathan came back on. "Mommy come too."

"That's not what I said. Give me the phone."

The sounds of a struggle ensued, then thudding and a breathless Nathan came back on. "I locked in bathroom. Mommy mad." Heavy pounding came next.

"Nathan Alexander, you open this door now!"

"Uh-oh. She use both my names. I in bigggg trouble." More pounding. "Lee-ah, I see Ker-sey. I help you find him."

"If you really saw him, can you tell me anything else about what was around him?"

"Yuh."

She waited. When he didn't respond, her irritation grew. She snapped. "Then tell me."

"Don't yell at me, Lee-ah. Mommy yelling enough."

She fought down the rising anger and frustration. In a controlled voice, she said, "Can you tell me?"

"Yuh"

Nothing more. She slapped her face with a palm. "Then, please tell me."

"Long buildings. Fences. Water. Lots and lots of water. Really big boat."

"You mean like a dock or a harbor? You know what a harbor is?"

"Yuh."

"Can you see if he's there now?"

"No. Still dark."

"Uh-oh. Mommy here. Gotta go."

The line went dead.

CHAPTER TWENTY-SEVEN

Did he really see Kersey? Did he really have a power? Was the boy somehow connected to Kersey? She had no idea, but for the moment it was the best lead she had. The only lead she had. She started the motor and shot from her parking spot.

Twenty minutes later, she was knocking at Nathan's door. The curtain moved at the front window. A female voice called from the interior. "Who is it?"

"It's Aleeyah. It's urgent that I speak with your son."

"Why?"

"Look, I'd rather not shout this in the open. Can we speak inside, please?"

The door cracked open. Two eyes and a forehead peered out. "This is not a good idea. I don't want Nathan involved. He's already too wound up and acting out. Please go and leave us alone."

She started to close the door, but Aleeyah's hand shot out and kept it open. "I understand your concern. I do. But Kersey's life is at stake. He is being held by the Russian mob."

That comment elicited a gasp from Janelle.

"That's right. The same mob that kidnapped Nathan. I believe this is retaliation for us bringing down this mobster's brother. They will be brutal. You don't want that for Kersey, do you?"

"No. Of course not. But I also don't want it for my son."

"I understand, but it's imperative I speak with him in case he knows anything else."

"You can't possibly believe he had a vision of where Kersey is?"

"Yes. I do. I think your son has an ability that neither of us can comprehend. Besides, at this moment, it's the only lead I have. Please."

"I, uh, I just don't think this is a good idea."

"Neither is standing by while Kersey gets tortured and killed. He dropped everything, including me, to answer your call to stay with Nathan. You owe him. If he hadn't come back here, he'd never be in this position."

"That's unfair."

"Maybe so, but it's all I've got."

Janelle bit her lower lip as she thought. "Okay, but just for a minute. Then you leave. Understood?"

"Yes. And thank you."

She stepped back and widened the space for Aleeyah to enter. Nathan was sitting at the dining room table writing on a piece of paper. As Aleeyah got closer, she noticed he was writing numbers from eleven to twenty.

"Nathan?" his mother called. "You have a visitor."

He whirled in his seat, saw Aleeyah, and bounded from the chair. "Lee-ah!" He wrapped his arms around her. "You come for me."

Aleeyah gave a nervous glance to Janelle. "Ah, I came to talk to you."

"But I help find Ker-sey."

"That's what I want to talk about. Have you seen any other pictures of Kersey?"

"No. Still dark."

"Can you remember anything else about the area? I need to narrow down the location."

"You're telling me you actually believe Nathan saw Kersey?" Janelle gaped.

"I believe it, and I'm praying it's true."

"How is that possible? That's something out of a TV show."

"I don't question how. I just know there are certain things that exist in this world that for the moment are beyond our comprehension." She knelt next to Nathan. "Do you see anything at all?"

He closed his eyes and furrowed his brows, then shook his head. "No."

Aleeyah's phone rang. It was her contact. She pushed to her feet and walked away from Janelle and Nathan. "What have you got?"

"What I've got is the makings of a bonus I was promised."

"Give and we'll see."

"I've got three possible."

"Send them to me."

"On the way."

"Owiee, Mommy. Owiee."

"What's wrong, Nathan?" Janelle bent in front of her son. His hands were on his face.

"Face hurts. Owiee." He pulled his hands away and stared at them with frightened eyes. "Blood, Mommy. Face bleeding."

"Nathan, you're scaring Mommy." She shook him.

"No!" yelled Aleeyah. "Let him finish." She hurried to his side. "Go on, Nathan. What else do you see?"

If he heard, he gave no response. His eyes were glazed over and his vision somewhere far off.

"What's happening to him?"

Aleeyah said, "Shh!" then added, "He's in the middle of a vision."

Janelle looked pale, her concern for Nathan growing by the second.

"Bear. Big Bear. Hitting Kersey." His head swung back then wobbled. Aleeyah recognized the motion as someone who'd been struck and has no control over their body. Kersey was being beaten and he was on the verge of unconsciousness.

CHAPTER TWENTY-EIGHT

Nathan snapped out of his trance moments later. He looked dazed. He saw his mother and erupted into tears. They embraced and held each other close.

"Oh, Nathan! Are you all right?"

"Yuh." He sniffled, wiped his nose on his sleeve, then pushed away from his mother. His eyes locked on Aleeyah's. "Bad men beat Ker-sey. Dark again."

"What was that about a bear?"

Nathan held his arms out in a shrug. "I saw bear hit Ker-sey."

"A real bear?"

He shrugged again. "Don't know. It look real." He raised his arms and formed his fingers into claws and growled in a deep voice. "Big bear. Mean."

Aleeyah's phone buzzed with an incoming message.

As she opened it and read, Janelle said, "You can't possibly believe this is real?"

Aleeyah held up a finger. Janelle kept talking.

"There's no way. He can't have ESP or something like that. That stuff isn't real."

Aleeyah read from the phone. "Big Bear Shipping. Private dock three miles out of the city along the coast." She turned it so Janelle could read. "No, the bear wasn't real. He was seeing the sign with the name of the company where Kersey is being held."

Janelle's jaw dropped open. She glanced from the phone to Nathan, then to Aleeyah. "This isn't possible."

"For Kersey's sake, you'd better hope it is."

While Lee-ah and his mother talked, Nathan went upstairs to find his Super Me costume. His mother made him take it off before dinner, but now he needed it again. He pulled of the Mickey Mouse shirt. He still wore the black sweatpants with the torn knees, then searched the room and his drawers for the costume but couldn't find it. He went to the clothes hamper and found it wadded up on top. He pulled it out and let it unwind. It was wrinkled and dirty. He put it to his nose and sniffed. He pulled back and made a face. "Pee Uee." He went into the bathroom, found his mother's perfume that he was never supposed to touch, and gave each underarm a spritz. Now it not only smelled better, but it smelled like Mommy.

He squeezed into the shirt and admired himself in the mirror. The yellow shirt with the bright red S and the red cape hanging down the back made him smile. "Look good, dude," and gave himself a thumbs up before going down stairs.

He jumped the last step, stumbled, then righted himself, placing hands on hips and posed. "I ready. Let's go save Ker-sey."

"Oh no. You march yourself right back upstairs and take that outfit off. I never should have made it for you."

"No, Mommy. I Super Me. We go save Ker-sey." He looked at Lee-yah for support.

"It would be helpful to have him with me in case of another vision."

"No. No way."

"Way, Mommy."

"You stay out of this!" she snapped at Nathan. She squared up with Lee-yah, but before she could unleash the verbal assault she intended, Lee-yah held up a hand. "You come too. Sit in the back seat with him. When we get to our destination, you stay in the car. I'll leave you the keys. If trouble starts, you get away from there."

Janelle's jaw line tightened. Her glare hardened. Again, she was about to unload on Lee-yah, when Nathan stepped between them and took her hands. "Come on, Mommy. Ker-sey in trouble. He my friend. He your friend too. Friends help friends."

Dumbfounded, Aleeyah acted quickly. "Great idea." She grabbed both of their hands and led them toward the door. Janelle dragged her feet. Aleeyah was out of patience. She tightened her grip on Janelle's hand, about to yank her through the door, when she said, "At least let me get my purse."

With relief, Aleeyah released her. A minute later, they were in the SUV heading toward Big Bear Shipping.

Along the way, Nathan tried several times to reconnect with Kersey, but said, "Still dark," each time.

Janelle questioned Aleeyah about her son's strange abilities. "Has he had this all his life? How did you know about it? Will it go away? Will it affect his life? Is there a way to control it?"

"Whoa! Slow down. I'm no expert. And I don't recommend that you have him tested. People will want to use him and control him if word gets out. Just keep it secret. I'm guessing the reason it's showing itself now is because of the tie that Kersey and Nathan have established. Perhaps it's enhanced because of the shared trauma they experienced last month. I just don't know. Accept that it's real and whenever he tells you something he saw, believe it."

"Believe it? I can't believe this. It's something right out of a-a ..."

"Comic book?"

"Yes. Exactly."

"Yuh. After we save Ker-sey, they write a comic book 'bout us."

"That's all I need."

Nathan covered his mouth and snickered. "You funny, Mommy."

"Why am I funny?"

"'Cause that not all you need."

"It's not? What else do I need?"

"Super Me."

All the fight, confusion, and worry disappeared for the moment. How could she argue with that?

CHAPTER TWENTY-NINE

Kersey woke but kept his eyes closed; not that they were in any condition to open at the moment. The mobster's goons took a lot of pleasure delivering blows that either erupted blood or swelled his eyes shut. It did make pretending to be out easier to pull off.

He had to come up with a plan. His body, though strong, had its limits. No one was built to accept this amount of punishment. He had to do something fast, or the mobster would bury him. His hands had been reinforced when they tied him to the chair. The chair itself had been nailed down. His feet were also secure. If he used his power to push off the floor now, he risked ripping his arms from their sockets.

It wouldn't take long for his abusers to come back for another round, so he had to make the best of the time he had available, but what could he do? A scraping sound made him more alert. He kept his breathing slow and soft, but with so much blood crusted inside his nostrils, it was a difficult task.

Footsteps echoed off the metal walls. Someone grabbed his hair and yanked his head back. Kersey offered no resistance. The man slapped his face twice, then let his head flop to his chest.

"He's still out," the man said.

Someone else said, "I'll give you some cash. Go grab us some food. We'll eat, then get back to work on our friend."

"Sure, boss."

The footsteps retreated. A door opened and closed, but Kersey now knew the others were in the room with him a short distance away. They'd be able to see any move he made. With one gone, now was the time to make a move. If he could get one of them behind him, he might be able to blast the man into oblivion. He needed to draw them to him one at a time.

He opened his eye a slit to gather information. A white strip of cloth had been wound tightly around his thigh to prevent him from losing too much blood. Without moving his head, he could not see how far away the men were. It didn't matter. He still had to draw one near. He was about to emit a low groan like he was coming out of his Russian-imposed coma, when the sound of an overhead door rising caught his attention. Beeping like that of a vehicle backing up followed. Engine noises grew. From the sounds of it, it was a diesel; perhaps a semi.

The door opened and greetings were exchanged. Kersey tried to determine the number of new arrivals. At least two, maybe more. His chances had just diminished. They spoke Russian at first, then the boss and one of the new men came closer and switched to accented English.

"So, this the guy who killed your brother?"

"Da."

"They never seem so tough after a little exercise, do they?"

The boss laughed. "No. He's about to get weaker still. We're taking a lunch break. I didn't want him to die too quickly."

"No. We wouldn't want that, would we?"

"Hey, big man. You still with us?" the boss said.

"Hey. He's talking to you." A kick landed below the back of his neck and ignited new pain and rocked him forward. He slumped against his bonds like he was still unconscious. "You sure he's not dead already?"

A hand grabbed his hair and pulled back his head. "No. See? He still breathes." Released, his head fell forward.

A kick was planted on his forehead, rocking him backward. He used the momentum and shoved hard against the floor. His head snapped back with a painful crack. For an angst-filled second, he thought he'd broken his neck. Slowly, feeling and movement returned.

"Easy now, Igor. Don't kill him before I get more pleasure from his pain."

"As you wish, my friend."

Footsteps faded away from him, leaving him to explore the potential of the now-loosened legs of the chair. Keeping his feet planted, he pushed hard to determine the extent of the space he had to work with. He guessed the nails driven into the concrete floor had risen more than an inch. How long were the nails? Were they nails or spikes? Kersey cracked an eye open to get a look at the floor, but without moving his head he had no angle.

In slow increments, he moved his head to the side until he could see the nail heads. He remembered when they were set. The installer used a .22 caliber Mastershot—essentially a .22 pistol to set the nails. If he remembered right, they could drive up to a three inch pin. If the nail rose an inch from the chair rocking, they must not be very secure.

He allowed the front legs to touch down, then leaned forward to lift the back legs. He couldn't be sure, but he thought the rear nails were out farther than the front. He strained against the nails. Had they moved? Too hard to tell. The only way to know for sure was to put enough pressure against them. However, to do so would be obvious to those around him.

Even if he got the chair free, his hands and feet were still bound to it. It might give him the chance to use his power blast, though, which might buy him time to waddle out of there. What he really needed was a distraction.

CHAPTER THIRTY

"Uh-oh," Nathan said from the back seat. "Lights on. Gonna be trouble."

"What do you mean, the lights came on? Did someone turn on lights in a room? Can you see the room?"

Nathan was silent. "Ker-sey awake. Face hurt. Eye not work."

"Can you see anyone near him?"

Nathan ignored her. He shouted, "Owiee! Owiee!" He rubbed the back of his head.

Janelle whipped around, hand already unfastening her seatbelt. "What is it, Nathan?" The high pitch of her voice told Aleeyah she was on the verge of hysteria. She glanced in the mirror to watch Nathan.

Janelle reached for her son, but he suddenly slammed backward into the seat, crying out again. His eyes rolled and Aleeyah feared he was unconscious. Did the boy feel the same pain that Kersey was going through? With what Kersey did for a living, she couldn't imagine a worse ability if he was tied by some extrasensory connection.

He shook his head, clearing his eyes. He appeared dazed, then said, "Bad man kick Ker-sey in face." He scrunched up his face in a mean glare and growled, "Grrr! They hurt my friend." He punched a fist into the opposite palm. "Bad men gonna pay."

"Nathan?" Janelle said, shocked at his tone. "Stop making that face."

"Lee-ah."

She glanced back.

"Drive faster."

Aleeyah did, deciding she liked this version of Nathan even better.

From Janelle's house the drive took a good fifty minutes. She took a turn as directed by the GPS and drove toward the water. At the end of the road was a closed gate. A guardhouse stood behind it to the right. She stopped before getting too close and searched for a turn-off. She found one that didn't seem to have a purpose. It ran parallel to the waterfront and was hidden from view by a row of trees. She caught an occasional glimpse of the chain link fence through gaps in the trees, then parked and scanned the area.

"Okay. This may be the best place to stop." To Janelle, she said, "Get in the driver's seat and be ready to move. If anyone comes, drive away." Janelle started to object, but Aleeyah grabbed her forearm and squeezed to emphasize her words. "Listen to me. If trouble comes, you go. If I'm not back in twenty minutes, call the police, but don't make the call from here. Get away."

Janelle inhaled to speak, but Aleeyah wouldn't allow it. "Hey! This is what we do. We're trained. You're not. If you want to protect your son, you drive away from here, and fast. Now get in the driver's seat."

She exited and Nathan opened his door. Aleeyah caught it and stepped in front of him. "You stay here, Nathan."

"No. I help save Ker-sey."

"You already have. Now it's up to me. You have to stay and protect your mom. Can you do that?"

He looked at his mother's worried face. "Yuh."

"Good man." She let him get back in the SUV and shut the door. As she turned to leave, the window rolled down.

"Lee-ah."

Annoyed, she looked back but kept moving.

"Big room. Big truck. Lots of bad guys."

She nodded. "Good to know."

She ran through the trees. Thirty feet later, she stopped and crouched at the tree line. In front of her were two large steel constructions running lengthwise, side by side toward the water. She studied the guardhouse. A head in the window appeared to be moving to the beat of a song. Down the fence to the right was another gate. It was smaller and had no guard. She moved toward it. She stopped, scanned the length, then broke for the fence. She didn't want to attack, afraid the ripples might extend down the line too far. She reached it and toed to the top before flipping it. She stuck the landing like the gymnast she had been many years ago.

As soon as she touched down, she angled for the far end of the building. Around the corner, she pressed to the corrugated steel wall and took a quick peek. No one followed. She ran the length of the building and stopped at the far corner. She saw there were actually four buildings. All looked the same. The only differentiating mark was the large number painted at the apex of each roof. She wished she'd asked Nathan which building Kersey was in.

As she watched, a black Cadillac limousine pulled up to the building marked with a four in front of her. A man exited, carrying an assortment of fast food bags. He kicked the door, unable to open it with his loaded arms. A large man pulled it open.

"What took you so long? I'm starved."

"Next time you go get it, then."

Both men had Russian accents. She was in the right place. Now she had to find a way in. A long scan showed the way clear. She darted across and continued down the length of building four and peered around the corner. The cab of a semi was sticking out of a bay. That meant workers might be close. Time was short. She couldn't afford to look for other ways inside.

Aleeyah crept toward the open overhead door, pulling her Smith and Wesson 40 cal from the holster at her back. At the opening, she knelt and peered in at ground level. The angle she had of the interior was clear, but the majority of the building was blocked by the trailer. She moved to the first set of tandem wheels and got a good view of the right side of the building.

It was large and wide open. Pallets holding large cardboard boxes wrapped in clear film stood against the far wall. Nothing else was stored inside. A rectangular folding table had been set near the door on the front side. Six men sat around it, eating. Was that all the men? And where was Kersey?

She duck-walked to the middle set of wheels. Still no sight of him. At the back wheels she ducked under the trailer. A ramp had been placed at the open rear and blocked her from being seen. Aleeyah crawled to the left and sighted over the ramp near the floor. Slumped and bound to a chair was Kersey. He appeared to be unconscious. She watched him for a few seconds and noticed the back two legs of the chair rise so slow it was almost imperceptible, which was obviously the intent. It rose and stopped. The cords of muscle in his back tensed. He was not only secured to the chair, but the chair was fastened to the floor.

The chair slowly lowered. She stuck her head out a little farther to make sure no one else was lurking somewhere. Once she made her presence known, she didn't want any surprises. She slid her Benchmark knife from her pocket, and with a practiced move, flicked and locked the blade open.

Taking one last look, Aleeyah stepped from cover, gun raised, and moved toward Kersey as she'd been trained. She crouched slightly, trying to keep Kersey between herself and the table. Halfway there, one of the Russian goons crunched up his food bag, stretched his arms over his head, and issued a burp loud enough to echo throughout the structure. Looking up, he caught movement, swung his head toward Aleeyah and said, "What the—"

Aleeyah had to reach Kersey before shooting started. She ducked behind him, sliced through the ropes and tape at his wrists with one powerful swipe, then pressed the knife into his now free hands.

She stood and shouted at the men rising from their chairs. "Stay down! Don't make me shoot! Stay where you are!" Her voice was strong and commanding. The group froze, but only for an instant. Then they scattered and reached for weapons. Chairs flew, the table toppled, and guns appeared.

Aleeyah fired twice, taking out the nearest man. Behind her, Kersey grunted from his efforts. They must have really worked him over or he'd have been free already. She tracked the next target and pulled the trigger. Another thug spun and went down, but she was pretty sure he was only wounded. She had to move to be less of a target, but she didn't want to leave Kersey unguarded.

He stood, took two steps, then fell next to her. She glanced down. By the time she looked for her next target, something was pressed to the back of her head. She swallowed hard. The next second would tell if she lived or died.

"You will drop the gun, please, or I will coat the floor with your blood."

She lowered the gun to the floor and released it. Aleeyah didn't need a gun to be deadly, but she had to be alive to do anything. As she stood, the gun jammed into her back, pushing her forward.

"You must be the woman who helped this man kill my brother. I can't tell you how happy I am to meet you and not have to track you down."

CHAPTER THIRTY-ONE

Another vision swept through Nathan's mind. Ker-sey was awake. Through his eyes Nathan saw Lee-ah walk toward the bad men with a gun. She was really a cool superhero. He smiled. The bad men were gonna get it now.

Then, Ker-sey felt pain in his head and he fell. This time, Nathan didn't cry out. As the moving picture in the building went dark again, he knew two things. Ker-sey and Lee-ah were in trouble, and he was the only superhero left to rescue them. He opened the car door, jumped out, and ran before his mother could stop him.

"Nathan! You come back here right now!"

He kept running.

"Nathan!" He recognized the tone as her angry voice.

"Sorry, Mommy," he said loud enough only for his ears.

He broke through the trees and ran along the fence toward the gate. He stopped behind the guardhouse where the steady drone of loud music thrummed. The guard had not noticed him. He ducked and moved to the gate. Nathan looked up. It was high, but not as high as his window. He could fly over it. He extended his arms upward and willed himself to lift off the ground, but nothing happened. He jumped. That didn't work. He said, "Fly." He still didn't take to air, but the sudden lowering of the music made him squat and move behind the guardhouse again.

The man in the uniform stood and glanced through the windows on each side of the shack. The seconds ticked by with a slowness that taxed Nathan's patience. He wanted to move. Every fiber in his body protested the lack of movement. Then, the music filled the guardhouse again and Nathan released a long, loud breath.

Back at the gate, Nathan studied the ten-foot-high fence. Why couldn't he fly? He was doing something wrong. Then it came to him. He had to be up high first and then jump. He remembered floating above the ground. The thought made him smile. "Yuh," he said and placed his fingers through the links.

Another memory came rushing back. Lee-ah said he couldn't fly. A moment of doubt crept through him. The top of the fence seemed a long way up. But an image of Ker-sey in pain and bleeding pushed the fear aside. He stuck his shoe into a lower link and pulled up.

His first step slipped. He tried again, determined to fly to Ker-sey's and Lee-ah's rescue. He got halfway up when he heard his mother. "Nathan. No!" He glanced her way. The music lowered again and the guard stood. Nathan had to hurry. His fingers were getting tired and sore, but he pushed on.

The guard spotted his mother and stepped from the shack. He watched her for a moment until Nathan's body cast a shadow over the man. He whirled, hand reaching to his belt for the gun holstered there, but he did not pull it free.

"Hey! What are you doing? Get down from there."

Nathan didn't answer. His hand wrapped around the top crossbar and he chinned to the top. The guard moved to intercept him.

"Boy, this is private property. Get down, or you'll be in trouble."

Nathan grunted as he put both arms over the top. "No."

"No? What do you mean, no? Get down or I'm gonna have to knock you down."

"Have to save Ker-sey."

"Who? Ain't nobody with that name here. What, are you pretending to be some sort of superhero?"

He placed a foot on the bar. "Not pretend. I Super Me."

"Okay, sure. If you say so, but you still can't come in here. Now, climb down."

"No. I fly." Nathan shoved off the top bar and went airborne.

"Nathan!" his mother screamed.

"What the—?" the guard said.

The smile never left Nathan's face as he soared up, then straight down. He landed on top of the guard, knocking him to the ground. His head snapped back, connecting with the concrete. His body bounced once, bucking Nathan off. Nathan rolled stopped and sat up feeling dizzy. When the ground stopped moving, he saw the guard was still lying on the ground.

Nathan threw his arms up and shouted. "Yuh!" He got to his feet, a little shaky at first, and took off running toward the water.

"No!" his mother shouted as she reached the gate. "Nathan, come back here. Please!"

"I save Ker-sey and Lee-ah." He stopped for a moment and smiled back at his mother. "Mommy, did you see? I flied." Then he took off running and disappeared between the two buildings.

Janelle could take no more stress or anxiety. The surgery, one she now regretted, had left her unable to chase and catch Nathan. She didn't wish to think, much less talk about it. She felt Kersey was on the verge of asking but was relieved he didn't. How had everything gone so wrong so quickly? The answer was that she let Kersey back into Nathan's life. Well, she'd had enough. She pulled out her cell phone and called the police.

She gave a detailed account of what was going on and where she was, but before the operator could say more, she disconnected.

Then, like any desperate parent would do to save their child, she started climbing the fence.

CHAPTER THIRTY-TWO

The four standing men moved in, all with guns aimed at her. Without moving her head, she shifted her eyes to Kersey's prone body, praying he was playing possum.

The wounded man rose to his feet, issued a slew of curses, and charged at her, one arm dangling at his side. He burst through the four gunmen and launched a punch at her face. Behind her, the man yelled, "Dimitri, stop!" but he was beyond being able to hear or stop.

Aleeyah watched the fist close the distance to her face in slow motion from outside her body. She waited until the last second, then simply moved her head. The punch zipped past. Unable to stop his momentum, he connected with the gun hand.

In a blur, Aleeyah, snagged the gun hand, snapped the gun down and twisted, freeing it from her opponent's hand. Fearing a reflexive shot from one of the four gunmen, she spun behind the wounded man, ducked, and came up with her arm wrapped around his throat and the gun pointed at the now-unarmed shooter.

"Everyone remain calm, and no one has to die," she said. She took a quick assessment of the man she held at gunpoint. Since he had been behind her, she hadn't seen him. Judging by his suit, she guessed he was in charge. "Especially not your boss." She eyed the men as they spread out. Without taking her eyes from them, she cocked the trigger. "Stop, or the first bullet enters his right eye." They complied for the moment. "I'm going to leave here with my partner."

"No, you are not," the boss said. His dark eyes bore deep into Aleeyah's face. The hatred she saw there was palpable.

"You'll be the first to die."

He smiled. "If she does not hand me the gun, shoot her partner."

Two of the shooters changed their aim to Kersey.

"Now what?" the boss said. "We shoot him, you shoot me, they shoot you. You die."

"So do you."

He shrugged. "Maybe yes, maybe no."

Aleeyah gritted her teeth. She wanted very much to put a bullet into the smirking face, but what he said was true. Any way she played it, she and Kersey ended up dead. She tried to think of a way to use her ability, but though telekinesis was a great skill to have, it was also limited. With the four gunmen spread out as wide as they were, she couldn't affect them all at the same time. She needed to find something as a distraction, but even then, how could she get Kersey to safety before the bullets started flying?

She had to do something fast. The gunman to her right inched another side step, giving him a good line of sight at her body. If only Kersey would wake and lend his considerable talents. The tension mounted with each passing tick of time. She took a quick scan of the building, searching for something to use as a distraction. Just a quick turn of the head was all she needed to gain an advantage.

When the distraction came, however, her heart sank like a dropped bomb.

"It Super Me to the rescue!"

The familiar voice echoed throughout the space. Nathan stood in his classic pose, fists on hips, chest thrown forward, head back. He stood proud, ready to take on the world to save his friends.

As one the four guns turned, Nathan backed up, startled by the sudden attention. One of the gunmen broke the trigger and the bullet spewed forth. Nathan stumbled back then toppled in a flurry of red.

"No!" Aleeyah screamed, but it wasn't her voice she heard.

"Nathan!" Kersey rolled to his back and drove Aleeyah's knife deep into the boss's thigh. He leaped to his feet and clubbed the first gunman as he was turning back. Kersey struck him so hard that he appeared to break in half like a board cracked over a knee.

As the boss danced around on one foot bellowing over his wound, the man she held snapped his head back, catching her in the side of her face. Fury flared. She gripped the man's throat and pulled him sideways, spinning him away. As he came around to face her, she leaped up and came down with the pistol butt, slamming it into his face. The skin on the forehead split, the nose flattened, and blood spurted. He dropped like an anchor. She looked for her next target.

Kersey reached the man who shot Nathan. Rage consumed him and filled the room with a force of its own. He swatted the gun aside as it fired, then shot his hand forward to wrap around the man's throat. He squeezed tight enough to crush the larynx, then lifted him effortlessly above his head and dropped to one knee, smashing the man into the ground. The back of his head broke like a dropped watermelon.

Though the man was surely dead, Kersey slammed his limp body twice more.

Aleeyah used her power to lift the third gunman's hand as he fired at Kersey. Then she fired her own gun at the fourth man who was turning to engage her. Two shots plowed through his body, ending his threat. As the third gunman swung her way, she triggered two more rounds into him. With both men down, she walked forward and placed one final round into each man's head.

Kersey tossed the seemingly boneless body twenty feet away and ran to Nathan. He got to him just as Janelle entered the building. She screamed, "Nathan!" and rushed to his side. Kersey beat her by a second, but as he reached for Nathan, Janelle shoved him aside and yelled, "Get away from my son!"

Her words stung. He withdrew his hands and said, "Don't move him until we can see what his injuries are."

Janelle glowered at him but did not lift Nathan to her as she'd intended.

Nathan looked from one face to another and said, "Owiee!"

"Oh, Nathan, are you all right?"

"No, Mommy. Cape too long. Catched my foot. Make me fall."

The three onlookers displayed confused looks, then Aleeyah burst into laughter. Janelle and Kersey glared at her. "Oh, lighten up, you two. He got his feet tangled in the cape and fell. He's not hurt, are you Super Me?"

"No. Not hurt. Angry at cape."

"See? There's no blood. Just an occupational hazard."

Kersey breathed out with relief. Janelle grabbed Nathan and lifted him to her chest, pressing him tight.

"Mommy. Squeeze me too tight."

They all laughed then.

CHAPTER THIRTY-THREE

Sirens grew louder but were still in the distance. Janelle looked at Kersey. "I called the police. I wasn't taking any chances with Nathan's safety." Her tone was defiant, daring him to give protest.

He nodded and stood, moving away from mother and child to give them space. Aleeyah followed. "You should go before the police get here."

"We should both go," she replied.

"No, I can't risk any of them," he motioned to the Russians, "getting away. I won't leave Janelle and Nathan to answer questions alone. Besides, I've done nothing wrong. I was the victim. But you don't need to be here. The authorities don't need to know you were ever here."

"It's better if we both leave." She nodded toward Janelle. "Unless there's another reason for you to stay."

He sighed. "No. Whatever thoughts I'd entertained were nothing more than wishful thinking. There's nothing for me here. I was a fool to believe otherwise."

She put a hand on his arm. "Normal lives and relationships are not meant for people like us."

He frowned. He wanted to argue with her, but he knew she was right.

"For what it's worth, I'm sorry."

She started to move away but Kersey snapped a hand out and caught her arm. "No, Aleeyah. For what it's worth, *I'm* sorry."

Their eyes locked and held. She nodded.

"Thank you for coming to my rescue."

She flashed one of her brilliant smiles. "What are partners for?" He released her. "We'll talk later. I'll keep the old phone for twenty-four hours. After that, well, it was nice while it lasted." She winked and jogged toward the rear door, disappearing around the semi.

He would call well before the allotted time. They were a good team. He'd be a double fool if he let that end.

The sirens were louder now. Nathan was on his feet and Janelle guided him toward the door. He watched, not wanting to intrude on their moment. Nathan looked back. "Ker-sey. Come. We tell police about being superheroes."

Oh boy! He needed to convince Nathan not to say too much. He trotted up next to them and stopped. "We need to talk about this."

"I'm not lying to the police," Janelle said with stern finality.

"I'm not asking you to. I'm only asking that you please don't mention Aleeyah was here. She doesn't need to be caught up in this."

"Neither does my son, but once again you managed to place him in danger."

He opened his mouth to defend himself, but the hard glare in her eyes convinced him it was futile. He hung his head.

Silence expanded the distance between.

"All right. I won't lie, and I won't mention your friend unless I have to."

"Thank you."

"You understand, Nathan? We don't mention Aleeyah."

"K." He nodded and reached for Kersey's hand. "We save the world, huh?"

"Yes, Nathan. We saved the world."

"Not Nathan. Super Me."

"That's right. Super Me saved the day. You saved me too. Thank you, Nathan."

"You should have see me, Ker-sey. I flied."

The statement took Kersey by surprise. "Flied? You flew?"

"Yuh."

Kersey looked at Janelle.

"He climbed the fence and jumped down. He thinks that was flying. Is that something else you taught him to do? Am I going to have to worry about him jumping off things?"

"Nathan, I told you about that. You can't really fly. You have to stop doing that, or you're going to get hurt."

"No hurt. I superhero."

Kersey squatted and took Nathan's arms. "Nathan," he said in a firm voice. "Don't you ever try to fly again. You hear me? This is very important. No more flying—or I won't come and visit you again." He didn't look at Janelle. He doubted he'd ever be allowed to see Nathan again anyway.

"Ker-sey." Nathan placed a hand under Kersey's chin and lifted. "You go away again?"

"Yes, I have to." He was surprised to find his throat constricted. "I have to work."

"You come back? See me?"

"Not if you fly."

A tear welled in one eye. His lip quivered. "Okay. Promise. No flying." He wiped at his eyes with his forearm. "You come see me?"

"Yes. When I can. If your mother says it's all right." He risked a glance. Her eyes were still cold. She didn't speak.

He stood as the first police car came into view. It had been a mistake to come back. He hoped the decision wasn't about to cost him his freedom.

CHAPTER THIRTY-FOUR

The bureaucracy that was the police department moved in slow motion. Kersey was taken by ambulance to a local hospital where surgery removed the bullet and repaired his leg. Once out of recovery he was grilled separately from Janelle and Nathan. The doctor waved the detectives away after thirty minutes, saying his patient needed rest. After being assured by the doctor Kersey was in no condition to travel, they informed Kersey they'd be back the next morning.

He called Janelle to make sure she and Nathan were all right. They had been released hours before. A long silence stretched out for an uncomfortable eternity before Janelle asked, "Are you going to be okay?"

"Yes. Doctor says I'll be up and around in a few days."

"That's good." More silence. Then they both spoke in a rush. They stopped and Kersey said, "You go." In his heart, he already knew what she was going to say.

"Though I'm truly thankful you came to watch Nathan, I can't do this anymore. Please understand and respect my wishes."

His throat tightened and he couldn't swallow or speak.

"Kersey?"

He cleared his throat. "Yes. I hear you and I'll respect your wishes."

"Thank you. Get well soon—and-and stay well." She hung up.

Later that night after the nurse made her rounds, he called a cab, dressed, and snuck out of the hospital. The cab was waiting and took him to his vehicle. Key in hand hovering above the key hole, Kersey debated whether to drive away or stop and say goodbye. He opted to drive away, but as he sat at the corner ready to turn right, his body disobeyed and he turned left. Despite his promise to Janelle, he had a question that needed an answer. At least that was the excuse he used.

He parked in the driveway, no longer concerned with anyone spotting his ride. On the front porch, he hesitated. The question spun around in his head, gaining momentum. The more he thought about it, the more he really wanted an answer. Before he could knock, the door opened and Nathan ran into his arms.

"Ker-sey."

Nathan rushed into his arms and held fast.

"You come back to see me."

"Of course, I did. What kind of friend would I be if I didn't stop to say goodbye?"

Janelle came up behind him. She did not look anywhere near as happy to see him as Nathan.

"I'm sorry to bother you. I know I'm not your favorite person, right now—or maybe ever, but something has been bothering me and I wanted to ask Nathan."

Janelle nodded, but made no motion for him to enter. Nathan grabbed his hand and dragged him inside. Before he allowed his foot to cross the threshold, he asked her, "Is it okay?"

She hesitated but nodded. He entered and closed the door.

"What did you want to know?"

"Well, I was taken to a place I didn't know. I left no clues, yet somehow you found me. I wanted to know how."

The question caused Janelle to stiffen; a curious response. "Why don't you ask your lady friend?"

"I will if I see her again. But, she's very good at what she does..."

"Whatever that is."

"Ah, anyway, if she was the one who found me, she never would have brought Nathan along. It's just not the way she operates."

She stared but did not reply.

"So, how did Nathan—or any of you, for that matterfind me?"

Janelle averted her gaze. Something troubling crossed her eyes before she broke eye contact.

"Janelle? What is it? What happened?"

"I-I don't know." Her voice was faint; afraid. Then it grew stronger. Angry. "I don't know and I don't want to know. If you did something to Nathan that made him..." She stopped abruptly, tears filling her eyes. She turned her head for a moment then returned her glare to him. "Ask your girlfriend. Just leave Nathan out of it. To say it was a mistake to trust you with my son would be a gross understatement. Please don't call or contact us again."

Her tone and her words made Kersey's neck hairs bristle. His hands clenched and unclenched. He started to speak, swallowed the angry retort, and tried again. "You called me. I'm sorry that things went off track—"

"Off track?"

"But I would never do anything to hurt Nathan—or you. This happened because I defended your son against some meatheads who called him names. You don't want me in your life, that's fine, but don't prevent me from seeing or talking to Nathan once and a while. I like him." He realized his voice was getting louder. He took a deep breath searching for a calm he did not feel. "Please. I'll always call first. Just short visits."

"Why? Why should I let you near him?" Her tone softened. "Why is he important to you?"

A good question. He looked down at Nathan. The boy smiled up, looking from his mother to Kersey. "I'm not sure I can explain it. I don't know for sure. But I like your son. I like you. You're good people, and in my line of work, I don't often get to meet good people. Perhaps if for only a moment, it makes me feel like a normal person. I'm sorry. I shouldn't ask. You have your son's best interest at heart. I can't fault you for that." He smiled at Nathan, who scrunched up his face and smiled back. "Just—think about it, please. I'll call maybe next week and you can tell me what you decide." He waited, hopeful for a positive response.

"I'll think about it."

"Thank you."

He squatted so he was face to face with Nathan. "I have to go now."

"To save the world?"

Kersey laughed. "Maybe. Remember what we talked about. Listen to your mother and no more flying."

"Aw man."

"You promised. And when a superhero makes a promise, he keeps it. And you're a superhero, right?"

"Yuh." He struck his pose. "I Super Me."

"Yes, you are. And I'm Super Me too."

"Yuh!"

He gave Nathan a big hug and said goodbye. He wanted to hug Janelle, but knew that'd be pushing it, so he smiled and waved. She didn't wave back, but he wanted to believe she had a smile in her eyes.

CHAPTER THIRTY-FIVE

An hour out of town, he called Aleeyah.

"Thought you were in the hospital."

"Chose early dismissal."

"Everything go all right with the police?"

"So far. Another reason for a premature exodus."

"So, guess this means we're still partners."

"If it's all right with you, I wouldn't have it any other way."

"Say your goodbyes?"

"Yes."

"Got it out of your system now?"

He knew she was asking more about Janelle than Nathan. "Yes."

"Good. We need to meet. Got a new job. You in?"

He gave a final thought to Nathan and Janelle before saying, "Let's do it."

They decided on a meeting place, then silence hit the airwaves.

"Aleeyah, how did you find me?"

He heard the sigh. "You sure you're ready to hear it?"

"Does it have something to do with Nathan?"

"The truth is, I had a working list and would've found you eventually. It was Nathan who zeroed in on your position. I found you on the first try, which is probably why we're able to have this conversation."

"What do you mean, he zeroed in on my position?"

"I'm not sure how to explain it. It was like he saw a picture of you. He described the location. I crossed checked it from my list, and there you were."

"He saw the location?"

"Not only that. He seemed to feel your pain. I think he has some sort of psychic connection to you."

"Seriously?"

"'Fraid so."

"That could be really bad."

"Indeed. Especially if he feels pain every time you get hurt. As often as that is, the kid may be in for some tough times."

"Very funny."

"I hesitated telling you this, because I know how you think."

"Meaning?"

"Meaning that you will try to avoid pain to prevent him from feeling it. To do that will make you tentative, which in turn puts our clients and us in danger. You're going to have to decide if you can still do this. Use the time it takes to get here to think it over. But Kersey, when you get here, if you're in, you're in all the way. Otherwise, it's time for me to move on."

"Understood."

Aleeyah sent a text with the coordinates. Kersey plugged them into his GPS and began the long drive.

Could he continue doing this work, knowing it might be hurting Nathan? Maybe the better question was, did he *want* to continue doing this work? Aleeyah was right about one thing. If he kept on in this profession, a normal life would never be his. Did that matter?

Only one way to find out.

Other Titles

Random Survival Series

Random Survival
The Long Search For Home
The Endless Struggle
The Journey to Normal
Then There'll Be None

Danny Roth Series

Teammates
Teamwork
Home Team
Stealing Home
Group Therapy

The Dead Series

Tower of the Dead

Island of the Dead

Escaping the Dead

Pick-A-Path Series

Pick-A-Path: Apocalypse 1

Pick-A-Path: Apocalypse 2

Pick-A-Path: Apocalypse 3

Stand Alone Titles

Warriors of the Court

Live to Die Again

Ghost of a Chance

Mischief Magic

Short Stories

The Con   Short Stop-A Danny Roth short   Super Me   Super Me, Too

Co-authored with Jason J. Nugent

Escape: The Seam Travelers Book 1

Capture: The Seam Travelers Book 2

Book 3 (Dec)

Find these titles, upcoming shows, appearances, and recent
newsletters at raywenck.com

www.ingramcontent.com/pod-product-compliance
Lightning Source LLC
Chambersburg PA
CBHW071924220626
47052CB00002B/446